THE WORLD OF EMILY DICKINSON

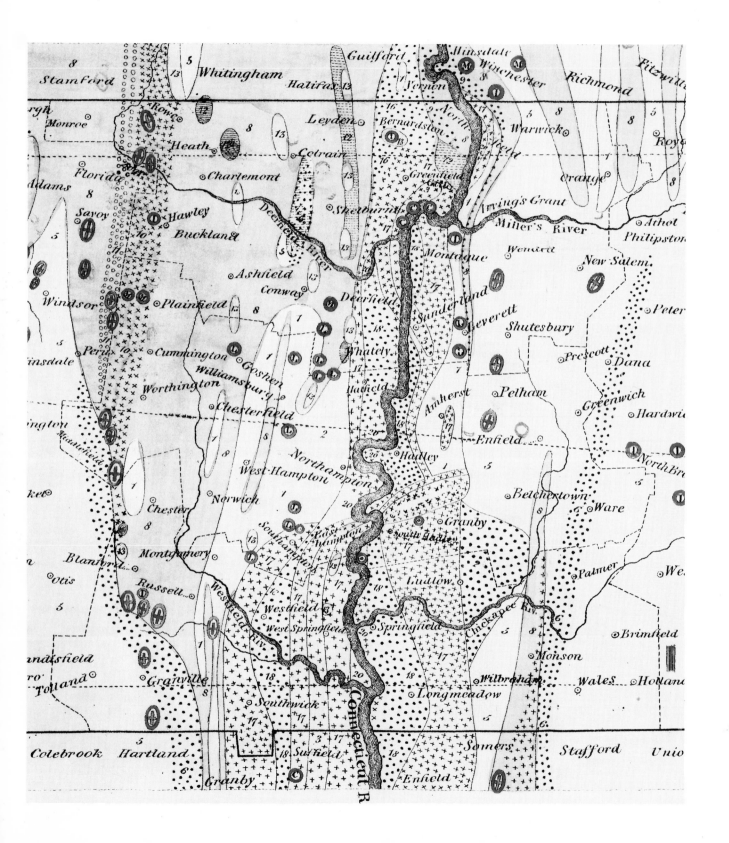

POLLY LONGSWORTH

THE WORLD OF EMILY DICKINSON

Emily Dickinson

W·W· NORTON & COMPANY   NEW YORK · LONDON

Dedication

For Nick, Charlie, and Tom, *in absentia*

First Edition.

Library of Congress Cataloging in Publication Data
Longsworth, Polly.
The World of Emily Dickinson / by Polly Longsworth.
p. cm.
ISBN 0-393-02892-5
1. Dickinson, Emily, 1830–1886—Pictorial
works. 2. Poets,
American—19th century—Biography—Pictorial
works. I. Title.
PS1541.Z5L64 1990
811'.4—dc20   90-31672

ISBN 0-393-02892-5
W.W. Norton & Company, Inc.
500 Fifth Avenue, New York, N.Y. 10110
W.W. Norton & Company, Ltd.
10 Coptic Street, London WC1A 1PU
1 2 3 4 5 6 7 8 9 0

Facing the title page.
Western Massachusetts,
including Amherst (east of
Connecticut River, *in center*).
Detail of geological map from
the plate book of Edward
Hitchcock's *Report on the
Geology of Massachusetts,*
1833.

CONTENTS

CHRONOLOGY

1 January 1803	Birth of Edward Dickinson, Emily Dickinson's father, in Amherst, Massachusetts.
3 July 1804	Birth of Emily Norcross, Emily Dickinson's mother, in Monson, Massachusetts.
6 May 1828	Marriage of Edward Dickinson and Emily Norcross.
16 April 1829	Birth of William Austin Dickinson, Emily Dickinson's brother.
3 April 1830	Edward Dickinson buys half of family homestead on Main Street from his father, Samuel Fowler Dickinson.
10 December 1830	Birth of Emily Elizabeth Dickinson.
19 December 1830	Birth of Susan Huntington Gilbert, Emily Dickinson's future friend and sister-in-law, in Greenfield.
28 February 1833	Birth of Lavinia ("Vinnie") Norcross Dickinson, Emily Dickinson's sister.
December 1833	S. F. Dickinson, bankrupt, leaves for Cincinnati, Ohio, after selling his half of family homestead to the Mack family.
4 August 1835	Edward Dickinson becomes Amherst College treasurer.
September 1835	Emily Dickinson begins primary school.
22 April 1838	Death of Samuel Fowler Dickinson in Hudson, Ohio.
April 1840	The Dickinsons move to North Pleasant Street after selling their half of the homestead to the Macks.
September 1840	Emily Dickinson begins attending the Amherst Academy.
5 May 1846	Death of Joel Norcross, Emily Dickinson's maternal grandfather, in Monson.
September 1846	Austin Dickinson enters Amherst College.
September 1847– August 1848	Emily Dickinson enrolls for one year at Mount Holyoke Female Seminary, South Hadley.
December 1849	Vinnie Dickinson enrolls for one term at Ipswich Female Seminary, Ipswich.
August 1850	Austin Dickinson and Emily Dickinson's friend George Gould graduate from Amherst College
11 August 1850	Admission of Edward Dickinson and Susan Gilbert to First Congregational Church by profession of faith. Vinnie admitted in November.
1850s	Emily Dickinson begins writing poetry.
17 December 1852	Election of Edward Dickinson to Congress
24 March 1853	Death of lawyer Benjamin Franklin Newton, Emily Dickinson's friend and literary mentor, in Worcester.
July 1854	Austin Dickinson graduates from Harvard Law School and is admitted to Massachusetts bar.
February and March 1855	Emily and Lavinia Dickinson visit Washington, D.C., and Philadelphia.
November 1855	The Dickinson family moves back to the repurchased and remodeled Main Street homestead.

1 July 1856	Marriage of Austin Dickinson and Susan Gilbert in Geneva, New York.
1858	Emily Dickinson begins practice of entering her best poems into fascicles.
Spring? 1860	Reverend Charles Wadsworth calls on Emily Dickinson in Amherst.
19 June 1861	Birth of Ned Dickinson, Emily Dickinson's nephew.
Early 1860s	Emily Dickinson undergoes an emotional crisis of unknown origin.
15 April 1862	Emily Dickinson first writes to man of letters Thomas Wentworth Higginson.
February– April 1864	Several Dickinson poems appear in *Drumbeat, The Round Table,* and *The Springfield Republican.*
April–November 1864 and April– November 1865	Emily Dickinson lives in Cambridgeport while consulting a Boston ophthalmologist.
29 November 1865	Birth of Martha Dickinson, Emily Dickinson's niece.
27 January 1866	Death of Carlo, Emily Dickinson's Newfoundland.
16 August 1870	Thomas Wentworth Higginson visits the poet in Amherst.
10 July 1872	Edward Dickinson resigns as treasurer of Amherst College after thirty-seven years.
5 November 1873	Edward Dickinson is elected to the General Court of Massachusetts.
1 December 1873	Austin Dickinson becomes Amherst College treasurer.
3 December 1873	Thomas Wentworth Higginson calls on Emily Dickinson a second time.
16 June 1874	Death of Edward Dickinson in Boston.
15 June 1875	Mrs. Edward Dickinson becomes paralyzed.
1 August 1875	Birth of Gilbert ("Gib") Dickinson, Emily Dickinson's nephew.
16 January 1878	Death of Samuel Bowles.
20 November 1878	Dickinson's poem "Success" is published in *A Masque of Poets.*
Late 1870s	Dickinson falls in love with Judge Otis Phillips Lord of Salem.
Summer 1880	Reverend Charles Wadsworth pays second call on Emily Dickinson.
31 August 1881	Mr. and Mrs. David P. Todd move to Amherst.
1 April 1882	Death of Rev. Charles Wadsworth.
14 November 1882	Death of Mrs. Edward Dickinson.
5 October 1883	Death of Gib Dickinson.
13 March 1884	Death of Judge Otis Phillips Lord.
12 August 1885	Death of Helen Hunt Jackson.
15 May 1886	Death of Emily Dickinson.
19 May 1886	Funeral of Emily Dickinson.
12 November 1890	Publication of *Poems by Emily Dickinson,* ed. Mabel Loomis Todd and T.W. Higginson (Boston: Roberts Brothers).
9 November 1891	Publication of *Poems by Emily Dickinson,* Second Series, ed. T.W. Higginson and Mabel Loomis Todd (Boston: Roberts Brothers).
21 November 1894	Publication of *The Letters of Emily Dickinson,* 2 vols. ed. Mabel Loomis Todd (Boston: Roberts Brothers).
16 August 1895	Death of Austin Dickinson.
1 September 1896	Publication of *Poems by Emily Dickinson,* Third Series, ed. Mabel Loomis Todd (Boston: Roberts Brothers).
March–April 1898	The Dickinson *versus* Todd Lawsuit.
3 May 1898	Death of Ned Dickinson.
31 August 1899	Death of Vinnie Dickinson.
12 May 1913	Death of Susan Dickinson.
14 October 1932	Death of Mabel Loomis Todd.

Opposite. Elijah Boltwood's tavern sign swung at the center of Amherst from 1806 to 1838.

INTRODUCTION

Asked at age thirty-one to supply a photograph of herself, Emily Dickinson replied, "Could you believe me—without? I had no portrait, now, but am small, like the Wren, and my Hair is bold, like the Chestnut Bur—and my eyes, like the Sherry in the Glass, that the Guest leaves— Would this do just as well?"

In clear defiance of her era's enthusiasm for photography, Dickinson chose words rather than an image to represent her, avoiding the camera as earnestly as she hid from public view and leaving only an oil portrait, a silhouette, and a daguerreotype, all made before she was twenty, to satisfy visual curiosity. The challenge for any picture book about this poet lies in the near absence of its subject.

Her invisibility demands some explanation. As a poet, Dickinson was supremely conscious of the power her words possessed to attract readers to herself, to bring the public to her door. She herself craved biographies and portraits of her literary favorites—the Brontës, the Brownings, George Eliot. The fame attendant on publishing her poems during her lifetime was abhorrent to her, not simply out of modesty, but as a consequence of "peculiarities" that afflicted her, whose specific nature is insufficiently delineated to diagnose.

Beginning about the time she started writing poetry, in her early twenties, Dickinson suffered a nervous condition that restricted her from what her contemporaries, and we, consider a normal life. Misunderstandings of the conditions and choices these circumstances imposed on her poetic career (and in her lifetime, lack of general awareness that she had a calling) provoked myths and mysteries that have dogged Dickinson's reputation since her poetry began to be published in the 1890s, following her death.

Probably the most astonishing decision she made was that of deferring publication during her lifetime, of apparently choosing, as time went by and her symptoms did not abate, to be a posthumous poet. A few of her poems were published anonymously during her lifetime—we know of ten, some of them picked up and reprinted several times—but only one or two appeared with her permission. Her preference was for circulating selected poems among close friends. At her death she left a legacy of nearly eighteen hundred poems and a thousand remarkable letters that were not published in their entirety until 1958.

The risks for earthly immortality must have seemed to Dickinson only as large as those for heaven: "If fame belonged to me, I could not escape her- if she did not, the longest day would pass me on the chase-" she told her friend Thomas Wentworth Higginson. She observed her literary masters well—Shakespeare, Keats, favorite books of the Bible—and knew that great poetry did not survive on personality or on temporality, so she avoided both. If she sometimes seemed scornful of peers who rushed to print ("Publication is the Auction of the mind of man"), she excepted those who wrote for a living, particularly women such as the Brontës and her friend Helen Hunt Jackson.

One cannot equate this poet's absence with lack of

Introduction

presence. Emily Dickinson withdrew, but within nineteenth-century Amherst, Massachusetts she lived a life as simple, compact, and powerful as any of her poems. She participated in the lives of her family and friends, and engaged with prominent members of her society. Her village was important to her, and is recognizable today to visitors with an eye to its enduring features.

"A village in the woods," one resident called it about the time Dickinson was born, in 1830. "Primal forests touched the rear of the college buildings; they filled up with a sea of waving branches the great interval between the village and Hadley; toward the south they prevailed gloriously, sending their green waves around the base and up the sides of Mount Holyoke; to the east, they overspread the Pelham slope; and they fairly inundated vast tracts northward clear away to the lofty hills of Sunderland and Deerfield. It was a sublime deluge."

In this isolated setting Dickinson's paternal forebears farmed, raised large families, and participated in politics and the evangelical church for four generations. Amherst's distinction from dozens of similar settlements in the fertile Connecticut Valley lay in its excellent academy, begun in 1814, and in its college, founded in 1821. Samuel Fowler Dickinson, Emily Dickinson's grandfather, took a lead in starting both institutions. He had nine children of his own needing instruction at the academy, while his zeal for a college that would educate indigent, pious students for the Calvinist ministry stemmed from the regional fear of creeping Unitarianism.

For settlers of the area there was one trinitarian Congregational church. Theirs was a lived religion, their God a personal God, creator of the magnificent panorama surrounding Amherst, but also the fearsome appointer of His elect. Waves of revival swept through the village; one's spiritual condition weighted life, powerful sermons were spoken, dread and praise were voiced through the mighty hymns of Isaac Watts.

Of the college and village in 1830, a contemporary student tells us:

The college buildings, two plain three-story brick dormitories and a substantial chapel, were in a row, facing the west, on the top of a hill at the south side of a parallelogram, on the west, north, and east sides of which were scattered the few houses constituting the village of Amherst. The old wooden Congregational meeting house stood a few rods to the west. "College Hill," so called, was steep, shaggy and treeless. The paths leading to it, on either side of the village common, were dusty and muddy by turns—the common was uneven and wet in spring, parched in summer, and bleak and forlorn in winter.

Emily Dickinson was barely three when her grandfather, bankrupted from having attached his livelihood to the crusade to establish Amherst College, was forced to leave his birthplace to seek opportunities further west. Emily Dickinson's father, Edward Dickinson, a young lawyer with a wife and three small children, stayed in Amherst, became treasurer of the young institution, and nursed its fortunes along with his own.

The college, then, was integral to Dickinson's world, and remained so throughout her life. In the early days its few faculty members, all ministers, enlarged the intellectual horizons of the community. Its students, taking their meals with Amherst families, became foster sons who, as they graduated and moved into ministerial and missionary posts around the country and globe, vividly extended the connections of those who lived in little Amherst. Later, the college's students were Dickinson's friends, and their libraries an important resource nourishing her intellectual gifts.

Although the village grew prodigiously during her lifetime, little change occurred during her child and girlhood. She lived, from ages ten to twenty-four, not in the family homestead on Main Street, but in a generous white clapboard dwelling on North Pleasant Street, adjacent to the village burial ground. The house, with its surrounding fruit and fir trees, many

Sketch of Amherst, 1834, looking north from Amherst College past the Boltwood home, *foreground,* and up the town common. By M. Blake.

of them set out by Emily's father and her brother Austin, provided the happy environment for a girlhood so pleasant Dickinson later said she would love it not to end.

Here her precociousness unfolded, her love for study centering on the rigorous offerings of the Amherst Academy. She took piano lessons, explored the hills, streams, and fields of the area in search of botanical specimens, and mourned friends swallowed by the graveyard. Her originality and wit were evident early, revealed in imaginative letters, compositions, and the spoofing fun of her valentines.

A simple social life revolved around college events, church meetings, and a great network of relatives whom Dickinson visited and was visited by over the years. Offsetting this were quieter, more static aspects of the village, which hung in the memory of Sue Gilbert, later Austin Dickinson's wife:

As the snow lay two or three feet on the level in those wintry days, Amherst, with no street lighting, no trolleys, no railroads, seemed to my youthful and perverse mind, animal spirits and vigorous habits, a staring, lonely, hopeless place, enough to make angels homesick. The lugubrious sound of he church bell still rings in my winter dreams.

At seventeen Emily Dickinson left the village for a year to attend Mount Holyoke Female Seminary in nearby South Hadley, where she came under the tutelage of the pious educator Mary Lyon. On her return, she entered a decade-long romantic period, reading prodigiously through the 1850s, establishing warm friendships, adopting and discarding literary models, and serving in secret an apprenticeship in writing poetry. The origins of her attraction to poetry are hidden, but apparently began with encouragement from her father's law student, Benjamin Franklin Newton, about the time she returned home from the year at South Hadley. Her friends were courting, marrying, and worrying about the state of their souls, while Dickinson was "dreaming a *golden* dream." She was also beginning to struggle with panics and anxieties that made such simple acts as attending church or answering the doorbell nightmarish and debilitating.

She wrote at night by candlelight, at the small writing table in her room, but ideas flooded in as well during the day's round of housekeeping routines. "I know," says her cousin Louisa Norcross, "that Emily Dickinson wrote most emphatic things in the pantry, so cool and quiet, while she skimmed the milk; because I sat on the footstool behind the door, in delight, as she read them to me. The blinds were closed, but through the green slats she saw all those fascinating ups and downs going on outside that she wrote about."

This vignette, probably from the early 1860s, catches Dickinson in the act of composing, transferring the quick of life and her thoughts onto scrap paper. The closed blinds perhaps protected the milk, perhaps protected her eyes, so sensitive to light they pained her considerably during this time. Her favorite cousin, Loo, eighteen or twenty years old, listened from the footstool behind the door because the poet required distance from her audience.

Emily Dickinson's "differentness" was remarked upon by many friends and acquaintances over time. To some she seemed unusual, other-wordly; to others odd, abnormal. Within her beloved family her idiosyncracies were accommodated, even by her authoritarian father, "too busy with his Briefs." Edward Dickinson did not insist, for instance, when his family visited him in Washington, D.C., soon after his election to Congress on the Whig ticket, that his eldest daughter accompany them, although a year later, during a second family trip in 1855, Emily was able to do so. In an insightful gesture, her father procured for her a Newfoundland, the breed so dear to the Romantics, whom she named Carlo. With her dog as escort, she continued to walk out for several years.

Much has been written about Dickinson's parents—the unobtrusive mother, self-abnegating, unintellectual, and dependent; the father remote, humorless, and severe, a leader of endless civic enterprises who lacked rapport with his children. Genius in a female child was not something easily understood by either Emily Norcross Dickinson, who "does not care for thought" or Edward Dickinson, who "stares in a curious sort of bewilderment though I speak a thought quite as old as his daughter." Despite tensions and misunderstandings, Dickinson loved her parents, and over time came to appreciate the pathos in their personalities.

More vital to her than parents, however, were her sister Lavinia, lifelong companion within the family homestead, and her brother Austin, who married and lived next door in the Evergreens with his wife Susan and their three children. Emily conversed with Austin; they shared an aesthetic sympathy. Sue's friendship and sound critical judgment were essential to

Emily's work, particularly in the late 1850s as Dickinson began to copy dozens of her finished poems into little booklets constructed by threading several pages of folded notepaper into sheaves. She may have formed her "fascicles," as they have come to be known, with an eye to publication, but more likely, in the opinion of Dickinson scholar Ralph Franklin, they were the poet's way of creating order from the myriad bits of scrap paper on which she composed her drafts.

Within these fascicles one finds the clearest evidence of an unidentified trauma that afflicted Emily Dickinson in the early 1860s. Turmoil is manifest in a change in handwriting, in the swift accumulation of poems, and in the poems' emotional content, the themes suggesting unrequited love. Someone is addressed as "Master," and speculation has involved two friends, the Rev. Charles Wadsworth and *Springfield Republican* editor Samuel Bowles. Dickinson's acquaintanceship by the early 1860s was wide, however, and not all of her correspondents are known. Other distresses than love may have been involved—her eye problem, for instance, grew severe enough that in 1864 and 1865 she lived in Cambridge with her Norcross cousins for two eight-month stretches while submitting to treatment by a Boston ophthalmologist.

The early 1860s, the period of the Civil War, was also the time when Dickinson established a relationship with Boston editor and man of letters Thomas Wentworth Higginson, whom she wrote in April 1862 to ask if he would become her "preceptor." This was a curious act. By 1862 Dickinson had found her voice and knew her power. She had little need of a "preceptor," but seemed to want an authorative literary voice to back up her refusal to publish. That same winter, she told him, editors had solicited her poems and been surprised by her demurral. She didn't mention that trusted friends had passed her poems anonymously to the press without permission, but that was happening too. While sending Higginson dozens of her finest poems, Dickinson begged him to tell her her faults, to assure her she wasn't ready to publish. Always baffled by his "eccentric poetess," Higginson complied. "You saved my Life," she later told him, and by way of thanks granted him two astonishing interviews at her home, in 1870 and 1873.

After 1865 (and the death of Carlo), Emily Dickinson's reclusiveness increased. She rarely if ever left the contiguous Dickinson properties, although she tended her flower garden in summer and led an active life within the homestead, in touch by letter and through numerous attentions with her friends and neighbors. The lives of her nephews and niece in the house next door, the busy doings of her several family members, her intensive correspondences, and her reading and writing absorbed her. Edward Dickinson's death in June 1874, an event that shook the entire village, sent reverberations through the family. A year afterwards Mrs. Dickinson became a paralytic invalid (from 1875 until 1883 Emily and Lavinia nursed their bedridden, elderly mother), and within a few years, as if a ban had been lifted, all three of Edward Dickinson's mature children became romantically involved. Lavinia had a courtly admirer, Emily fell in love with Judge Otis Lord, her father's close friend and a widower, and Austin succumbed to the charms of Mabel Loomis Todd, wife of the college's young astronomy professor, beginning a thirteen-year affair that alienated his wife and children.

"My friends are my 'estate.'" Dickinson once proclaimed. "Forgive me then the avarice to hoard them!" She sustained most of her friendships on paper, finding joy in the writing and receiving of letters, developing her prose style into an art form few correspondents have matched. In the last five years of her life the deaths of several people dear to her seemed to take their toll on her health. The loss of her mother, Judge Lord, Charles Wadsworth, and her youngest nephew were all blows from which she staggered, beset again and again by the one doubt never stilled, "Is Immortality true?" Her own death occurred on 15 May 1886, from Bright's disease, when she was fifty-five.

No one privileged to attend the poet's simple and unusual funeral ever forgot the sparkling spring afternoon, Thomas Wentworth Higginson's reading of Emily Brontë's "No coward soul is mine . . . ," and the startling but apt procession of her white coffin out the rear door of the Dickinson homestead, through the barn, cross-lots to the graveyard, carried by Irish workmen who had tended the homestead and Evergreens properties. "They carried her through the fields, full of buttercups, while the friends who chose, followed on irregularly through the ferny footpaths to the little cemetery," wrote Mabel Loomis Todd, who was to play a major role in the complex process of publishing Dickinson's poetry.

Masterful at riddles, delighting in telling the truth but telling it slant, Dickinson left behind her an inexhaustably fascinating puzzle. The known fragments of her life never come together, the genius of her words and thought never stops dazzling. "The Poets light but Lamps—/Themselves—go out—..." she wrote. And so she did, having done her utmost to keep readers from knowing anything about her.

The rich visual imagery that binds homeliness and profundity in Emily Dickinson's poetry was drawn from a specific landscape. Fascinated by phenomena of the natural world and human heart, her poet's eye and imagination roamed the region immediate to Amherst, where she spent her entire life. Restoration of the place's contextual elements is enabled by the work of contemporaneous artists such as Orra White Hitchcock, a prolific watercolorist, and John L. Lovell, Amherst's photographer from 1856 to 1905. The self-trained Mrs. Hitchcock was encouraged by her husband, who was both theologian and scientist, to render closely observed particulars of the countryside, while J. L. Lovell prided himself on keeping at the forefront of photo-technology. His enthusiasm for recording the same scenes again and again in order to supply Amherst College's student class books allows us to watch Dickinson's setting change over time.

The pictures that follow come primarily from Amherst College, The Jones Library in Amherst, The Houghton Library at Harvard University, and the Yale University Library, which house the largest caches of visual materials pertaining to Dickinson. Together with photographs supplied more singly by other institutions and individuals, they help reestablish Emily Dickinson's world.

Acknowledgments

A chief pleasure of this book rose from working with many enthusiastic Dickinson fans, who contributed materials, suggestions, and spirited help. At Amherst College, thanks go to John Lancaster, curator of special collections, Daria D'Arienzo, archivist of the college, and Deborah Pelletier, special collections and archives associate. At the Jones Library in Amherst, Daniel Lombardo, curator of special collections, and Marty Noblick, department assistant, shared their keen interest in Dickinson and extensive knowledge of Amherst's history. Melanie Wisner, reference assistant of the Houghton Library Reading Room, was an invaluable ally in selecting from the Dickinson collection at Harvard University. Rodney C. Dennis, curator of manuscripts at the Houghton Library, smoothed my way. In Yale University's manuscripts and archives division, Judith Ann Schiff, chief research archivist, and William Massa, public services archivist, aided passage through the Todd and Bingham photograph collections at New Haven.

There are others, some named within the text, to whom I am grateful for kind services. Special appreciation is due Sylvia DeSantis, librarian of the Monson Free Library, for recognizing Mrs. Emily Norcross Dickinson among a box of unidentified Norcross daguerreotypes; Professor Barton St. Armand of Brown University for generously sharing his glimpses of the Evergreens; Frank Ward, Amherst College photographer, always game for one more shot; Carol Birtwistle, curator of the Dickinson homestead, who permitted me to stay in the Dickinsons's back bedroom; and my dear friends Ann and George May, providers of shelter in Amherst on demand. Thank you!

Orra White Hitchcock's "Autumnal Scenery, View in Amherst," looks at the village from Pelham, on east. Lithograph from the plate book of Edward Hitchcock's *Report on the Geology of Massachusetts,* 1833.

An 1833 map of Amherst by
Alonzo Gray and Charles B.
Adams. The population of
Amherst was 2,631.

1830–1847

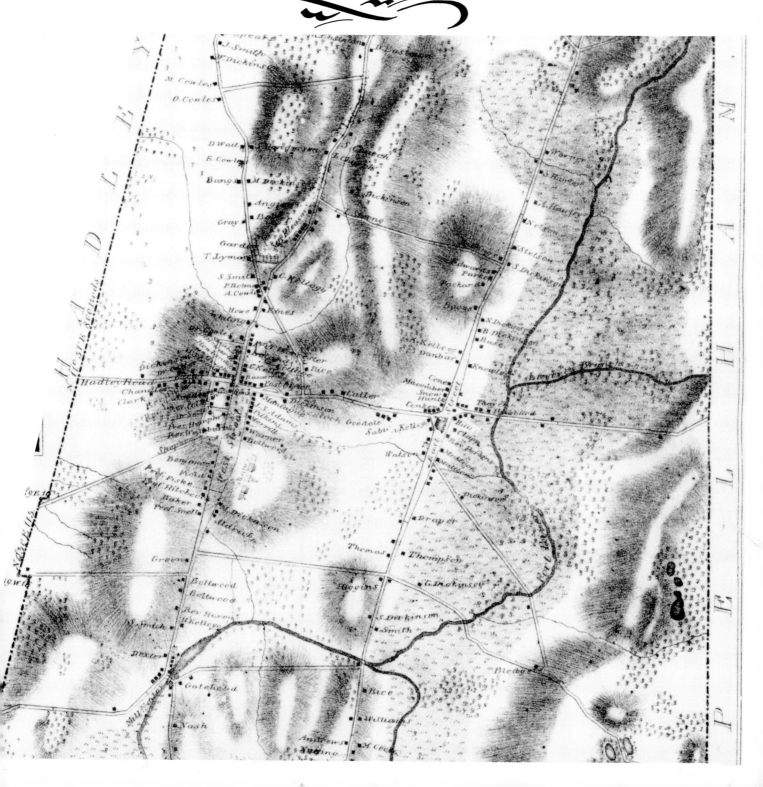

Emily Norcross Dickinson, Emily Dickinson's mother. Painted in 1840, when she was thirty-five, by itinerent artist O. A. Bullard.

Below left. Betsey Fay Norcross of Monson, Massachusetts, the poet's maternal grandmother. The mother of nine children, she died of consumption in 1829, the year before Emily Dickinson was born. Locket silhouette belonged to Emily Norcross Dickinson.

Opposite above. The Monson home in which Emily Norcross was born and lived until her marriage was built by her grandfather, William Norcross, ca. 1785. Originally a tavern, the second floor features a large ballroom. The second floor of the ell was added ca. 1835. The house still stands on Cushman Street, Monson.

Emily Dickinson's maternal grandfather, Joel Norcross, a prosperous merchant and farmer in Monson. Artist unidentified, n.d.

Joel Norcross's second wife was Sarah Vaill, *left,* the "Grandmother Norcross" the Dickinson children knew. She and Joel built the Greek Revival house shown *right* on Main Street, Monson, in 1835. The poet often visited here. Picture late nineteenth century.

Opposite above. The two-story frame house with half pilasters at the center of this 1875 photograph was Edward Dickinson's boyhood home. His father moved it to North Pleasant Street in 1813 when he built the brick mansion now known as the Dickinson homestead on his Main Street property.

Edward Dickinson, Emily Dickinson's father, painted in 1840 when he was thirty-seven by O. A. Bullard.

Opposite below. This 1840 lithograph of Main Street provides the earliest glimpse of the Dickinson homestead, *center background.*

Samuel Fowler Dickinson and Lucretia Gunn Dickinson, parents of Edward. Mr. Dickinson was a lawyer and farmer in Amherst. Edward, born in 1803, was the eldest of their nine children.

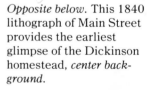

Opposite. With Noah Webster and other Amherst citizens, Samuel Fowler Dickinson played a prominent role in founding the Amherst Academy, *above,* in 1814 and Amherst College, *below,* in 1821.

Opposite below. Compiled by Mary Hitchcock from sketches made in 1821 by her mother, Orra White Hitchcock. South Dormitory, the first and for a time only college building, *on right. Left:* the village's Congregational Church *(second meeting house)* with its horsesheds.

Above. Amherst College student Joseph Howard made a camera obscura sketch before painting the same view in 1824. He omitted the unsightly horsesheds but included the Hitchcock home, *right foreground,* a new dormitory, and the bell that summoned students to class.

Reverend Heman Humphrey, president of Amherst College from 1823 to 1845, headed the small faculty whose piety, moral earnestness, and learning influenced village life during Emily Dickinson's girlhood.

Yale College as it appeared when Edward Dickinson entered, 1819. *Foreground:* the old burying ground on the New Haven green. Drawing by Baroness Hyde de Neuville, 1813.

Edward Dickinson's paper-covered Euclid copybook, made at Yale College his sophomore year, when he studied geometry. Because of his father's pecuniary difficulties, Edward spent the second term of his freshman year back home at Amherst Academy, and all of his junior year, 1821–1822, at the newly opened Amherst College.

Halfway through his senior year, for which he returned to Yale, Edward composed original verses for his classmates' albums. Here, as parting sentiment to Charles Stetson, student Dickinson expresses the desire "To penetrate each distant realm unknown/ And range excursive o'er the untravelled zone."

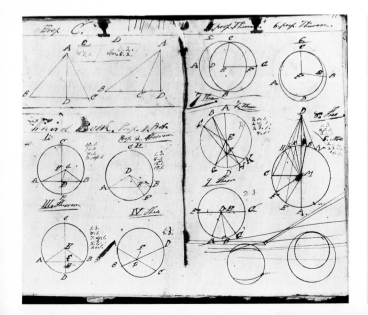

View of Monson, where Edward Dickinson courted Emily Norcross from 1826 to 1828. The Norcross homestead, distinguished by double hip roof and large cupola, appears *left foreground.* Monson Academy, where all the Norcross children were educated, is the steepled building, *center.* Painted by Erastus Salisbury Field, ca. 1820.

Emily Norcross Dickinson acquired the second edition of *The Frugal Housewife,* Lydia Maria Child's popular handbook of housekeeping, soon after her marriage. The volume contains recipes, remedies, instruction in economy, and moral advice for raising children.

After reading law in his father's office and attending Northampton Law School, Edward Dickinson set up his practice.

EDWARD DICKINSON,

ATTORNEY AT LAW,

HAS TAKEN AN OFFICE IN AMHERST,

IN THE NEW BRICK BUILDING

OVER "GRAVES AND FIELD'S" STORE, OPPOSITE "BOLTWOOD'S HOTEL,"

WHERE HE WILL ATTEND TO ANY BUSINESS THAT

MAY BE INTRUSTED TO HIM IN HIS PROFESSION.

AMHERST, (MASS.) SEPT. 1826.

74

COMMON CAKES.

IN all cakes where butter or eggs are used, the butter should be very faithfully rubbed into the flour, and the eggs beat to a foam, before the ingredients are mixed.

GINGERBREAD.

A very good way to make molasses gingerbread is to rub four pounds and a half of flour, with half a pound of lard, and half a pound of butter; a pint of molasses, a gill of milk, tea-cup of ginger, a tea-spoonful of dissolved pearlash stirred together. All mixed, baked in shallow pans twenty or thirty minutes.

Hard gingerbread is good to have in the family; it keeps so well. One pound of flour, half a pound of butter and sugar rubbed into it; half a pound of sugar; great spoonful of ginger, or more, according to the strength of the ginger; a spoonful of rose-water, and a handful of caraway seed. Well beat up. Kneaded stiff enough to roll out and bake on flat pans. Bake twenty or thirty minutes.

A cake of common gingerbread can be stirred up very quick in the following way. Rub in a bit of shortening as big as an egg into a pint of flour; if you use lard, add a little salt; two or three great spoonfuls of ginger; one cup of molasses, one cup and a half of cider, and a great spoonful of dissolved pearlash, put together and poured into the shortened flour, while it is foaming; to be put in the oven in a minute. It ought to be just thick enough to pour into the pans with difficulty; if these proportions

75

make it too thin, use less liquid the next time you try. Bake about twenty minutes.

If by carelessness you let a piece of short cake dough grow sour, put it in a little pearlash and water, warm a little butter, according to the size of the dough, knead in a cup or two of sugar, (two cups, unless it is a very small bit,) two or three spoonfuls of ginger, and a little rose-water. Knead it up thoroughly, roll it out on a flat pan and bake it twenty minutes. Everything mixed with pearlash, should be put in the oven immediately.

CUP CAKE.

Cup cake is about as good as pound cake, and is cheaper. One cup of butter, two cups of sugar, three cups of flour, and four eggs, well beat together, and baked in pans or cups. Bake twenty minutes and no more.

TEA CAKE.

There is a kind of tea-cake still cheaper. Three cups of sugar, three eggs, one cup of butter, one cup of milk, a spoonful of dissolved pearlash, and four cups of flour, well beat up. If it is so stiff it will not stir easily, add a little more milk.

CIDER CAKE.

Cider cake is very good, to be baked in small loaves. One pound and a half of flour, half a pound of sugar, quarter of a pound of butter, half a pint of cider, one tea-spoonful of pearlash; spice to your taste. Bake till it turns easily in the pans. I should think about half an hour.

ELECTION CAKE.

Old fashion election cake is made of four pounds of flour; three quarters of a pound of butter; four

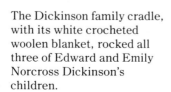

The "List of Women Delivered by I.G.C.," the nominal title of Dr. Isaac Cutler's record book, made note of only the fathers of newborns in Amherst. Emily Dickinson's birth on 10 December 1830 is eighth from the bottom. Fourth entry from the top is the birth of friend Helen Fiske, on 14 October.

Opposite. Portrait of the Dickinson children by O. A. Bullard, 1840. *From left:* Emily, William Austin (called Austin), and Lavinia. Emily and Austin inherited their father's red hair. Although the children did not resemble one another as closely as depicted, Bullard was thought to have caught Emily's expression well.

The Dickinson family cradle, with its white crocheted woolen blanket, rocked all three of Edward and Emily Norcross Dickinson's children.

Reverend Lyman Beecher, a prominent New England Calvinist pulpit orator, was president of Lane Theological Seminary from 1832 to 1850 and was the father of eleven children, including author Harriet Beecher Stowe, educator Catharine Beecher, and noted preacher Henry Ward Beecher, with whom he is shown here about the time Henry attended Amherst College. A friend of Edward Dickinson's younger siblings, Henry graduated in 1834 and often returned to the village to preach in later years. He was a trustee of the college 1866–78.

Samuel Fowler Dickinson, bankrupted by his efforts to start Amherst College, moved to Cincinnati late in 1833 to become superintendent of the year-old Lane Theological Seminary. There is no record of a prior relationship with Lyman Beecher, but Mr. Dickinson would have been familiar with the young institution's needs through Henry Beecher. With his wife and two youngest children, Emily Dickinson's grandfather lived in the Boarding Hall, *center,* and supervised construction of Kemper Hall, a dormitory, *right.*

Unable to make ends meet at Lane, Samuel Fowler Dickinson moved on to Western Reserve College in Hudson, Ohio, in 1836, where he served as treasurer. His sudden death from cholera in April 1838 at age sixty-two left the college's financial affairs in a muddle.

Emily Dickinson's Bible, a gift from her father in 1844, bears evidence of lifelong use. Here, turned corners in the Book of Revelation.

Below. Reverend Aaron Colton preached Calvinist orthodoxy from the village pulpit from 1840 to 1853. "No doubt you can call to mind his eloquent addresses, his earnest look and gesture, his calls of *now today-*" Dickinson reminded her brother.

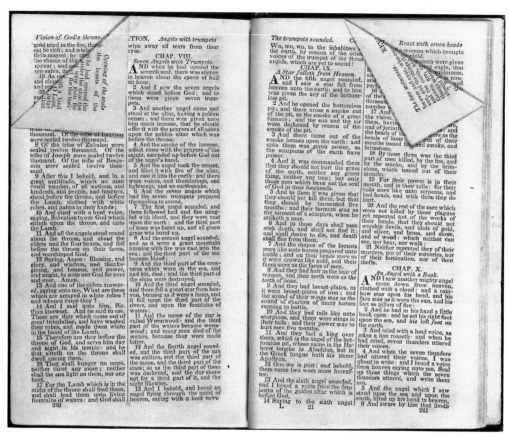

Opposite. The third meeting house of The First Church of Christ in Amherst, built in 1829, still stands on the corner of South Pleasant Street and Northampton Road, as it did when Emily Dickinson attended. Its portico was removed after Amherst College acquired the building in 1868; it was replaced early in the twentieth century with six columns.

Above. In 1840 this house on North Pleasant Street became the Dickinsons' home for the next fifteen years. At the time it had a central chimney, no gable, french window, porch, or second story on the ell, and must have resembled Edward Dickinson's boyhood home *(see p. 11, top).* The fence, too, is a later feature. Emily and Austin Dickinson always spoke fondly of this home. Picture ca. 1870

Right. The village graveyard lay alongside the North Pleasant Street property, on the northeast. From a north window, Emily watched funeral processions enter the main gate *(to left, out of picture).*

Above. "There was always such a Hurrah wherever you was," wrote Emily when Austin went to Williston Academy in nearby Easthampton in 1842, This is her earliest extant letter.

Executed by Charles Temple, a native of Smyrna.

1845

Emily E. Dickinson

Opposite above. The town's district school on North Pleasant Street, probably attended by the Dickinson children in their primary-school years.

Opposite middle. Emily Dickinson's childhood chair.

Opposite below. Austin Dickinson, ca. 1845, at approximately sixteen years of age.

Above. Silhouette of Emily Dickinson at age fourteen, cut by an Amherst College student from Turkey the year he graduated. To earn extra money, Charles Temple also instructed in French at Amherst Academy, 1843–1844.

Norcross family portrait, believed to be Emily Dickinson's cousins Emily Lavinia Norcross and her brother William, the orphaned children of Mrs. Dickinson's eldest brother, Hiram. From 1836, Emily L. Norcross lived with her grandparents, Sarah Vail and Joel Norcross, in Monson. Later she and Emily Dickinson were roommates at Mount Holyoke Seminary.

Samplers bearing versions of the same verse suggest the friendship between cousins Emily Dickinson *(sampler on left)* and Emily Norcross *(sampler on right)*. It lasted until Emily Norcross's death at age twenty-four.

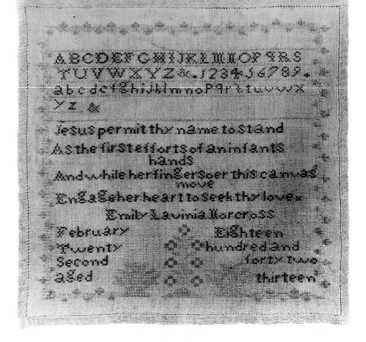

Amherst Academy, *right,* provided Emily Dickinson with a sound and stimulating education between 1840 and 1847. One principal remembered her as "a very bright, but rather delicate and frail looking girl; an excellent scholar . . ." whose "compositions were strikingly original."

Although she later gave it up, Dickinson's bound collection of waltzes, marches, quicksteps, and other sheet music attests to her girlhood pleasure in playing the piano.

Epiphagus americana. 13.2.

Betonica. 16.16.

Cypripedium spectabile. 14.2.

Chrysanthemum, parthenium. 17.2.

Opposite. The herbarium Dickinson made while studying botany at the Academy, and later at Mount Holyoke Seminary, holds over four hundred Latin-labeled flower specimens, most from the vicinity of Amherst.

Girlhood friends included Abiah Root, *upper left;* Mary Warner, *upper right;* Helen Fiske, *lower left;* and second cousin Sophia Holland, whose death in April 1844 led Dickinson into "a fixed melancholy."

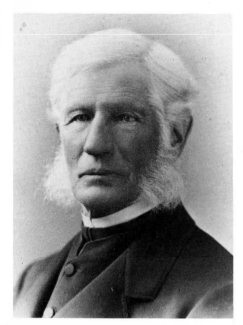

Dickinson relatives the poet knew best included *(top left and middle)* Uncle Asa Bullard and Aunt Lucretia Dickinson Bullard of Boston. Bullard was secretary and general agent of the Massachusetts Sabbath School Society. Uncle William Dickinson *(top, right)* was a prominent Worcester businessman. Mary Dickinson Newman and book publisher Mark Newman *(bottom, right)* died in 1852, leaving orphaned children. Edward Dickinson became guardian of the Newman girls. Later, Anna *(left front)* and Clara *(right front)* lived with Austin Dickinson's family.

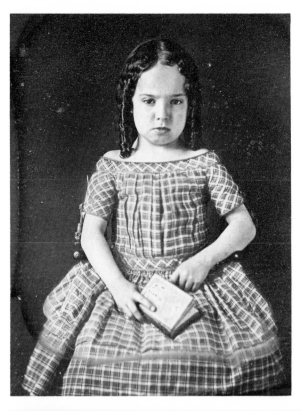

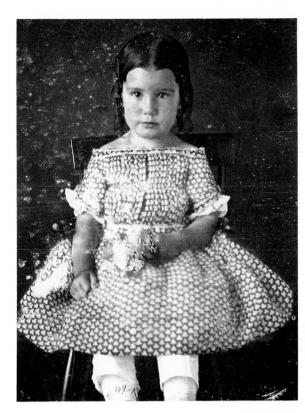

Two cousins who became Emily Dickinson's favorites were Louisa Norcross, *left,* and Fanny Norcross, *right,* daughters of Mrs. Dickinson's sister, Lavinia Norcross Norcross. Ca. 1850.

Above. A favorite aunt was Catharine Dickinson Sweetser of New York City. Her husband Joseph, a merchant, mysteriously disappeared in 1874.

Left. Aunt Elizabeth Dickinson Currier of Worcester, Edward Dickinson's youngest sister. "The trees stand up straight when they hear her boots," Emily commented.

The homes of Amherst friends and
neighbors Mr. and Mrs. Luke Sweetser
(*above,* 1856) and Mr. and Mrs. Lucius
Boltwood (*below,* ca. 1885). Mr. Sweetser was a principle dry-goods merchant
in Amherst, while Mr. Boltwood, a
lawyer and Free Soil Whig like
Edward Dickinson, was a leading man
of affairs. His wife, a magnetic talker
and formidable social force in the village, was cousin to Ralph Waldo
Emerson.

Orra White Hitchcock used her home and family as subjects for the frontispiece of husband Edward Hitchcock's book *A Wreath for the Tomb*. Here, in 1839, Dr. Hitchcock is greeted by his family after a journey. Jane (Jennie) Hitchcock, the little girl in front, became Vinnie Dickinson's best friend.

Edward Hitchcock's dinosaur tracks in Triassic sandstone slabs at the Ichthyology Collection, Amherst College. A natural theologist as well as an early geologist, Hitchcock inspired lively interest in the sciences in Amherst.

Above. William Bartlett's "View from Mount Holyoke," published in N. P. Willis's *American Scenery,* 1840, brought excursionists to the 800-foot-high peak south of Amherst. Senator Charles Sumner claimed that the prospect from its summit surpassed the Highlands of Scotland and Mont Blanc. Emily Dickinson climbed with friends to the mountain house, *left,* at least once, signed the guest register, and looked at the ox bow in the Connecticut River below.

Opposite above. The first Amherst College building designed by an architect was the octagonal natural history cabinet and observatory, depicted here by Orra White Hitchcock against the college's three dormitories and one classroom building, Johnson Chapel. From Edward Hitchcock's *Religious Lectures on Peculiar Phenomena in the Four Seasons,* 1850.

Opposite below. Growth in Amherst can be noted by comparing this view of the village, painted from Pelham ca. 1850, with the view on p. 5. Artist unknown.

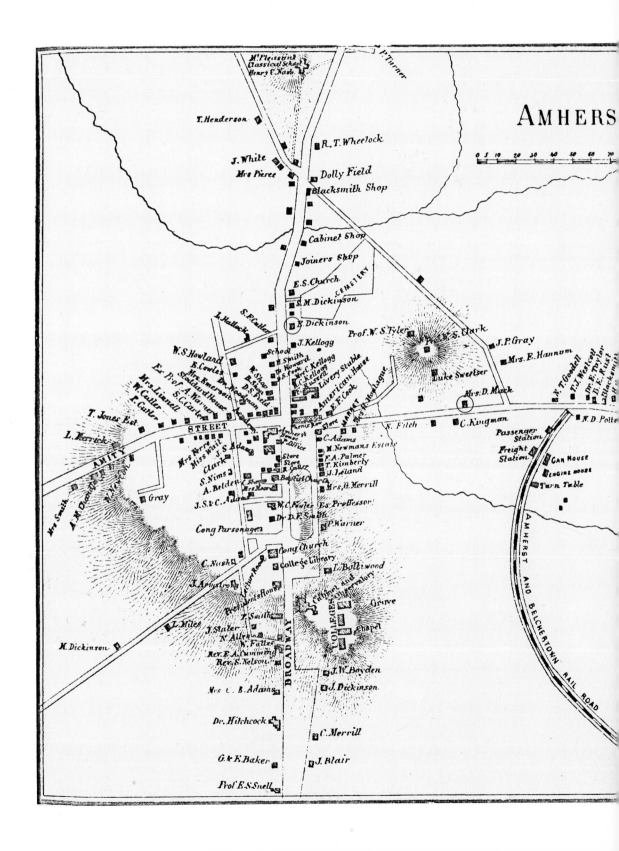

AMHERS

Mt Pleasant
Classical Scho
Henry C. Nash

T. Henderson

P. Turner

R. T. Wheelock

J. White
Mrs Pierce

Dolly Field

Blacksmith Shop

Cabinet Shop

Joiners Shop

E. S. Church

S. M. Dickinson

CEMETERY

E. Dickinson

0 5 10   20   30   40   50   60   70

L. Hallock   S. F. Cutler
W. S. Howland
E. Cowles   Dr. Nelson
Mrs Emerson   E. Shop   E. Smith
Ex Pro' A. Warner   S. Cook   B. Howard   Mrs C. Kellogg
Mrs Linnell   Stodard House   R. Shop   C. Kellogg
W. Cutler   S. C. Carter   D. S. Field   H. Russell
P. Cutler
T. Jones Est.

School   J. Kellogg

Prof. W. S. Tyler   A. S. Clark   J. P. Gray
Mrs E. Hannum
N. T. Goodell
T. J. Westcott
Dr. E. Taylor
B. E. Rust
Blacksmith

Luke Sweetser

Livery Stable
American House
E. F. Cook
M. S. Montague

Mrs. D. Mack

L. Kerrick

STREET

Mrs Smith   A. M. Dickinson   Temple Bar   Store
A. M. Dickinson   Amherst House   Office
AMITY   Mrs Kerr   Store   C. Adams
Miss Wait   J. S. Adams   Store
Clark   R. Cutler
S. Nims   Baptist Church
A. Belden   Mrs Noor
J. S. & C. Adams

N. Fitch   C. Kingman

N. D. Polte

Passenger
Station

Freight
Station

CAR HOUSE

ENGINE HOUSE

Turn Table

Gray

M. Newmans Estate
F. A. Palmer
T. Kimberly
J. Leland

Mrs. O. Merrill

W. C. Fowler   Ex Professor
Dr. D. F. Smith

P. Warner

AMHERST AND BELCHERTOWN RAIL ROAD

Cong Parsonage

Cong Church

C. Nash

College Library

L. Boltwood

J. Armstrong

Church Road

Cabinet and
Observatory

Grove

Presidents House

T. Smith

COLLEGES   Chapel

L. Miles

J. Slater
N. Allen
W. Fates
Rev. E. A. Cumming
Rev. S. Nelson

BROADWAY

M. Dickinson

J. W. Boyden

J. Dickinson.

Mrs C. B. Adams

Dr. Hitchcock

C. Merrill

G. & E. Baker

J. Blair

Prof E. S. Snell

1847–1860

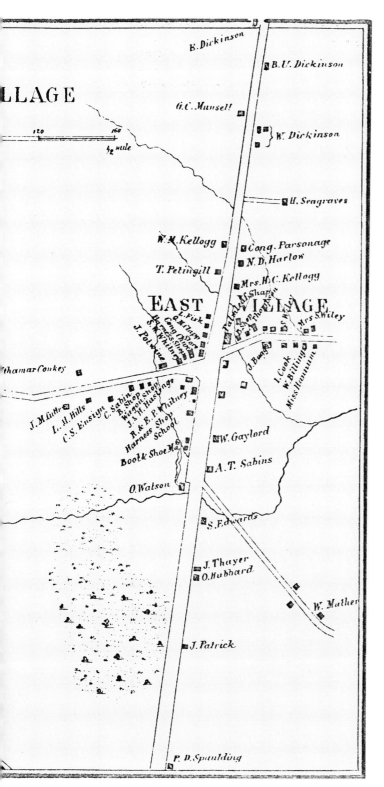

The Edward Dickinson family was still living on North Pleasant Street when this map of Amherst was made under the direction of H. F. Walling. By the time it was printed, in 1856, they had returned to the family homestead *(left)* on Main Street, occupied on the map by Mrs. D. Mack.

"I love this Seminary & all the teachers are bound strongly to my heart by ties of affection," Emily Dickinson wrote from Mary Lyon's Mount Holyoke Female Seminary in 1848. During her year there she experienced one of several revivals that touched her while she was young, though she was never persuaded to "become a Christian" and join the church.

On returning to Amherst, she entered the most socially active period of her life, forming new friendships and enjoying such pastimes as sleighing and sugaring parties, lectures, and a "reading society" in which she and friends read Shakespeare's plays aloud. About this time, she began to exhibit the increased timidity that gradually led to reclusive habits.

As early as 1850 Dickinson's intellectual precosity found an outlet in the writing of poetry, a vocation for which she began to train herself, largely in secret. She read widely among poets and prose stylists (she mentions Keats and the Brownings, Ruskin and Sir Thomas Browne, but prized Emerson, George Herbert, Jean Paul Richter, and Shakespeare as well), and she composed short verses employing what was most familiarly at hand—the language and cadences of the King James Bible, the rhythms of Isaac Watt's hymns and psalms—to describe her natural world and, through its emblems, explore religious themes, especially death and immortality. What distinguished her poems, even early on, were their economy and tension, their arresting first lines, and their wit. By decade's end enough finished poems had accumulated that she gathered 148 together into seven hand-stitched "fascicles."

Emily Dickinson attended Mount Holyoke Female Seminary in South Hadley during the school year 1847–1848.
Currier's lithograph of the seminary was drawn by student,
later teacher, Persis G. Thurston in 1844. It shows the
school as Dickinson knew it when she roomed with
her cousin Emily Norcross on the top floor.

The seminary's remarkable founder,
Mary Lyon, was careworn and tired
when her ferrotype was made in
1845, at age forty-eight. She died
suddenly in 1849, the year after
Dickinson was a student.

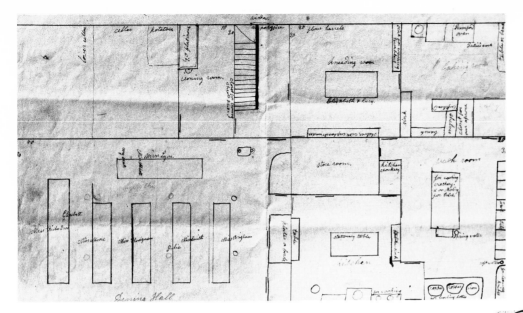

Floor plan of seminary basement, where dining room and kitchens were located, was sketched by student Lucy Goodale in 1838. Here Dickinson participated in the student work program by "carrying the Knives from the 1st tier of tables at morning & noon & at night washing & wiping the same quantity of Knives."

Above. Dickinson took botany, Latin, history, chemistry, and natural philosophy classes at Mount Holyoke Seminary. She loved all her subjects, but botany best.

Right. An abbreviated list of the seminary's rules, which were enforced by daily self-reporting. A black mark, or "exception," resulted when any were broken.

RECORDED ITEMS.

Absence from School Exercise,
Absence from Table,
Tardiness at School Exercise,
Tardiness at Table,
Tardiness in Retiring,
Tardiness in Rising,
Absence from Domestic Work,
Tardiness at Domestic Work,
Entering Rooms,
Communications of the first kind,
Communications of the second kind,
Failure in Walking,
Absence from Church,
Delinquency in Composition.

UNRECORDED ITEMS.

Spending time with others when it is not time for entering
Delay in the Space Way,   [Rooms,
Speaking loud in Space Way,
Interruption in Half Hours,
Specified time on Lessons,
Absence from Rooms in Study Hours,
Fire Laws,
Money Locked,
Rooms in order,
Entering or delaying in the Basement,
Silent Study Hours,
Closing Doors,
Loud Speaking after the Retiring Bell,
Conversing in Reading Room or Sem. Hall,

WEEKLY ITEMS.

Throwing things from the window,
Marking the Building,
Purchasing Eatables,
Setting or lying upon the Quilts,
Making things warm in Rooms,
Riding without permission,
Taking company to Rooms without permission,
Broken Crockery,
Calling at the Rooms of those not able to go to the Table,
Taking Tea out without permission,
Making calls without permission.
Exchanging Chamber Furniture or Bedding,
Taking any not given,
Lamps burning after retiring,
Sleeping with door closed,
Sending papers without permission,
Boxes of food,
Debts,
Rising before the Rising Bell,
Exposure of health,
Wardrobe in order,
Account Books balanced,
Time devoted to composition.

WASHING ITEMS.

Speaking above a whisper in the wash room,
Doing five minutes' work, or offering to do it,
Tubs rinsed,—Wash-boards in place,
Using pumps properly,
Changing circles without permission,
Omitting Washing without permission,
Passing over wet floors.

IRONING ITEMS.

Tardiness at the close of Ironing,
Putting flat on the Ironing Board,
Speaking above a whisper in the Ironing Room,
Carrying Holder and Duster,
Exchanging articles.

An unidentified friend cut a silhouette of the Dickinson family members when they called on Emily at the seminary in 1848.

Seminary Hall, the assembly room of the school, where devotions, talks by Mary Lyon, and public examinations were held. Picture from the 1870s.

Below. On 11 January 1848, Cousin Emily Norcross wrote to Mrs. Hannah Porter, wife of a seminary trustee, news of the religious revival at the school. Her roommate Emily Dickinson, she reported, remained among the "unconcerned." "She says she has no particular objection to becoming a Christian and she says she feels bad when she hears of one and another of her friends who are expressing a hope, but still she feels no more interest."

Daguerreotype of Emily Dickinson at about age sixteen. The same details of chair, book, and tablecloth appear in other daguerreotypes made at Amherst, suggesting that the likeness was taken there, rather than at South Hadley, as has long been supposed. This is the only known photograph of Dickinson.

Daguerreotype of Emily Norcross Dickinson, the poet's mother. The similarity
of pose and the use of the same props as the picture opposite make it likely
that the portraits were composed by the same photographer on the same
occasion.

In the 1850s Dickinson enjoyed friendships among the college students. *Upper left:* Austin Dickinson's commencement picture, 1850. *Upper middle:* Leonard Humphrey, Amherst College 1846, principal of Amherst Academy during Dickinson's last year there, and in 1849–1850 a tutor at the college. His death in November 1850 touched her closely. *Upper right:* George Gould's commencement photograph, 1850. *Lower right:* Dickinson's valentine, perhaps sent to George Gould, appeared anonymously in the student literary magazine, *The Indicator,* of which Gould was an editor. (Final paragraph of valentine omitted here.)

1850.]   *Editors' Corner.*   223

analyze it.—It is composed of nutgalls and copperas; but that is not what I want,—I don't want to know what it is made of, but what might be made of it.

So I mused, and not a word had I written, save

FEBRUARY, 1850!

"And savage winter rules the year."

February is indeed a cold rough personage, and were it not for St. Valentine's day we should be scarcely able to relax our features with a smile during his whole reign. Between the hilarity and pleasure of winter, and the anticipations of spring he stands; giving us no enjoyment except the knowledge that his reign is as brief as severe.

But St Valentine's day, although as rough as the blasts of Siberia, brings fun and frolic enough along with it, and this year brought *quantum sufficit* to us. Many a chary epistle did we receive, and many did we send—but *one, such* an one. I wish I knew who the author is. I think she must have some spell, by which she quickens the imagination, and causes the high blood "run frolic through the veins." Yes, the author, of such a gew gaw—such a frenzy built edifice—I should like to know and talk with, for I don't believe her mouth has any corners, perhaps "like a rose leaf torn!"

But I'll not keep you in the door way longer, but enter the temple, and decipher the thoughts engraved there.

ATTENTION.

"VALENTINE EVE.

" Magnum bonum, 'harum scarum,' zounds et zounds, et war alarum, man reformam, life perfectum, mundum changum, all things flarum ?

" Sir, I desire an interview; meet me at sunrise, or sunset, or the new moon—the place is immaterial. In gold, or in purple, or sackloth—I look not upon the *raiment.* With sword, or with pen, or with plough—the weapons are less than the *wielder.* In coach, or in wagon, or walking, the *equipage* far from the *man.* With soul, or spirit, or body, they are all alike to me. With host or alone, in sunshine or storm, in heaven or earth, *some* how or *no* how—I propose, sir, to see you.

" And not to *see* merely, but a chat sir, or a tete-a-tete, a confab, a mingling of opposite minds is what I propose to have. I feel sir that we shall agree. We will be David and Jonathan, or Damon and Pythias, or what is better than either, the United States of America. We will talk over what we have learned in our geographies, and listened to from the pulpit, the press and the Sabbath School.

" This is strong language sir, but none the less true. So hurrah for North Carolina, since we are on this point.

" Our friendship sir, shall endure till sun and moon shall wane no more, till stars shall set, snd victims rise to grace the final sacrifice. We'll be instant, in season, out of season, minister, take care of, cherish, sooth, watch, wait, doubt, refrain, reform, elevate, instruct. All choice spirits however distant are ours, ours theirs; there is a thrill of sympathy—a circulation of mutuality—cognationem inter nos ! I am Judith the heroine of the Apocrypha, and you the orator of Ephesus.

" That's what they call a metaphor in our country. Don't be afraid of it, sir, it wont bite ! If it was my *Carlo* now. The Dog is the noblest work of Art, sir. I may safely say the noblest—his mistress's rights he doth defend—although it bring him to his end—although to death it doth him send!

The Gilbert sisters became close friends of Emily Dickinson. *Above:* two girlhood pictures of Susan Gilbert. *Lower left:* Harriet Gilbert Cutler, married to Amherst merchant William Cutler, in whose home the Gilbert sisters lived. *Lower right:* Martha Gilbert, ca. 1851.

Above. The center of Amherst at mid-century by local artist George A. Thomas. Shown are the Amherst Academy, *on rise, right,* the Amherst House, *hotel, center,* and to its right, the Post Office and commercial buildings on South Pleasant Street, called Merchants' Row.

Left. The Revival of 1850 brought seventy persons into Amherst's First Church by profession of faith on 11 August 1850, among them Edward Dickinson, Susan Gilbert, and Dickinson's friend Abby Wood. Shown here is a page of admissions for that date from a church record book.

1231	Edward Dickinson
1232	Mrs Charles Dickinson
1233	Edwin C. Fairchild
1234	Henry Green
1235	Cordelia B. Green
1236	Lucretia Green
1237	Harriet E. Goodale
1238	Betsey J. Green
1239	Susan H. Gilbert
1240	William Harkness

I presume you have heard from Abby, and know what she now believes. She makes a sweet girl christian, religion makes her face quite different, calmer, but full of radiance, holy, yet very joyful. She talks of herself quite freely. Seems to love Lord Christ most dearly, and to wonder, and be bewildered, at the life she has always led. It all looks black, and distant and God, and Heaven are near. She is certainly very much changed.

She has told you about things here, how the "still small voice" is calling, and how the people are listening, and believing, and truly obeying, how the place is very solemn, and sacred, and the bad ones slink away, and are sorrowful, not at their wicked lives,

but at this change time, great change. I am one of the lingering bad ones, and so do I think away, and pause, and ponder, and ponder, and pause, and do work without knowing why, not surely for this brief world, and more sure it is not for Heaven, and I ask what this message means that they ask for so very eagerly, you know of this belief, and fulness, will you try to tell me about it?

Opposite below. In her letter of 7 May 1850, Emily Dickinson described for her friend Abiah Root the revival's strength in the village, and her own continuing indifference: "I am one of the lingering *bad* ones. . . ."

Above left. Joseph Bardwell Lyman, Vinnie Dickinson's admirer, ca. 1850.

Above right. Lavinia Dickinson, 1852.

Right. Vinnie's 1851 diary reveals she did not lack for beaus. Late March entries record Joseph Lyman's last visit. They parted in romantic sympathy, but Lyman later married someone else.

March. **SUNDAY, 23.** 1851.

Attend church all day. Mr Coleman preaches in the morning, Tutor Edwards in the afternoon. Slept sweetly.

MONDAY, 24.

Walked with Jennie, met Austin & Joseph riding. Tutors Edwards & Showlson called, Joseph & Emeline went to walk

TUESDAY, 25.

Been dear & unhappy. Jennie Humphry called in the morning, Were singing since the afternoon with a large company, & Storm over in the house

March. **WEDNESDAY, 26.** 1851.
Letter from E. Coleman.

Walked with Joseph. Now he is gone! Attend meeting made calls, visited John Sanford. met Storms there. pour maple sugar. Joseph has gone, two years is a long time!

THURSDAY, 27.

E. Bellogs calls in morning. Were Sugaring with El Tyler & Mr Trombley, Misses Gilbert Hitchuil & Emma calls. Mr Bowdoin, Thompson took supper here. Kattie is

FRIDAY, 28.

Thompson is staying here. Recd a strange letter. Abby Wood called, Walked with Jennie, Were a party in Sweetser, came home with Rowland.

On 3 July 1851, Jenny Lind sang in Northampton. Mr. and Mrs. Edward Dickinson and their daughters drove through severe thunderstorms in the village's box stage to attend her concert.

The only building large enough to hold the two thousand people who came that night to hear the Swedish Nightingale was the First Congregational Church of Northampton, *left. Right:* the Hampshire County Courthouse, where Dickinson's grandfather, father, and brother all practiced law.

Opposite left. Wedding daguerreotype of Jenny Lind and accompanist Otto Goldschmidt, whom she married the following winter, during a three-month honeymoon in Northampton. *"Herself,* and not her music, was what we seemed to love— she has an air of *exile* in her mild blue eyes," wrote Dickinson after hearing her.

After teaching school and reading law in his father's office, Austin Dickinson attended Harvard Law School, housed in Dane Hall in Cambridge, from March 1853 to July 1854.

Austin Dickinson, ca. 1854.

Henry Vaughan Emmons, Amherst
College 1854, shared a literary
friendship with Dickinson. He
became a minister.

Susan Phelps of Hadley, fiancee of
Henry Emmons until she broke
their engagement in 1860, was
Dickinson's good friend as well.

James Parker Kimball, Amherst College
1849, gave her Oliver Wendell
Holmes's *Poems* before he
graduated. He, too,
became a theologian.

John Graves of Sunderland,
Amherst College 1853, a cousin
through the Gunn family, was a
favorite of Dickinson's.

Romances, marriages, and partings occupied Dickinson's girlhood friends through the 1850s. Emily Fowler, *left,* married New York City lawyer and businessman Gordon Ford, *right,* in 1854.

Mary Warner, *left,* married Edward Payson Crowell in 1861. Edward, *right,* was a lifelong professor of Latin at Amherst College.

Wedding photographs of Abby Wood and Amherst graduate Daniel Bliss. They married following his ordination in 1855 and immediately sailed to Syria to begin the mission school that later became The American University of Beirut.

Below. Phoenix Row, as the commercial buildings on Main Street were called, ca. 1856. This is an early outdoor photograph of Amherst, perhaps taken by photographer J. L. Lovell, who came to the village in late 1856 and set up his first studio upstairs in the Marsh Building, *right edge.*

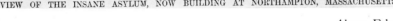

VIEW OF THE INSANE ASYLUM, NOW BUILDING AT NORTHAMPTON, MASSACHUSETTS.

Above. Edward Dickinson's civic and political involvements included the Northampton Lunatic Asylum, built in 1858, of which he was appointed trustee by the governor in 1859. *Left*. Thanks largely to the efforts of Edward Dickinson, the Amherst and Belchertown Rail Road began service in 1853, its 19½-mile line linking the village to major east–west and north–south rail routes in the state. Later the line's locomotive, which looked like the one portrayed here, was named for Mr. Dickinson.

Elected to the Thirty-third Congress, 1853–1855, Edward Dickinson defended military rather than civilian superintendence of the country's two national armories. His unpopular view occasioned his one speech in Congress and contributed to his defeat in the next election. Here, the United States Armory at Springfield in mid-century.

Emily and Lavinia Dickinson visited the capital for three weeks in February 1855, staying at the Willard Hotel, *left*. From the *Illustrated London News,* ca. 1853.

Cartoon by Emily lampooning for Austin their father's arrival in Washington, D.C., 1853.

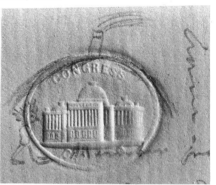

A popular visiting spot was George Washington's tomb. Like the Dickinson sisters, these tourists visited Mount Vernon in 1855.

During a two-week stop in Philadelphia on the way home, it is presumed that Dickinson heard the popular Rev. Charles Wadsworth *(above)* preach at his Arch Street Presbyterian Church *(right)*. They later corresponded, and he called upon her twice in Amherst, in 1860 and in 1880. Following his death she told a mutual friend, "He was my Shepherd from 'Little Girl'hood."

In April 1855 Edward Dickinson repurchased the family homestead. Lithograph by Bachelder, 1858.

Floor plans of the homestead, after Edward Dickinson's renovations in the summer and fall of 1855.

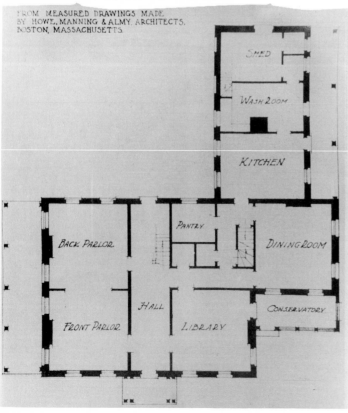

FROM MEASURED DRAWINGS MADE BY HOWE, MANNING & ALMY, ARCHITECTS, BOSTON, MASSACHUSETTS.

SHED

WASH ROOM

KITCHEN

BACK PARLOR.

PANTRY

DINING ROOM

HALL

CONSERVATORY

FRONT PARLOR.

LIBRARY

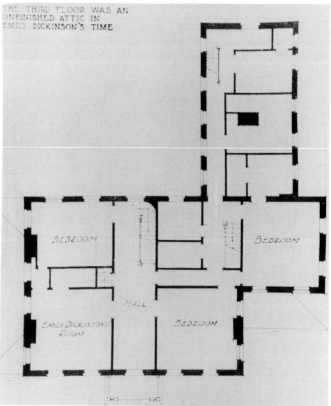

THE THIRD FLOOR WAS AN UNFINISHED ATTIC IN EMILY DICKINSON'S TIME

BEDROOM

BEDROOM

HALL

EMILY DICKINSON'S ROOM

BEDROOM

Nothing was wasted. Older, discarded elements of the house were incorporated into new sections of cellar wall.

The cupola Edward Dickinson added atop his house provided a 360-degree view through eight windows.

The great barn behind the homestead, sketched from memory by Austin Dickinson's daughter Martha Dickinson Bianchi in 1939. Inside were a carriage, sleigh, and harness rooms, and stalls for two horses and two cows. The barnyard held a pig, hens, a well, and a pump.

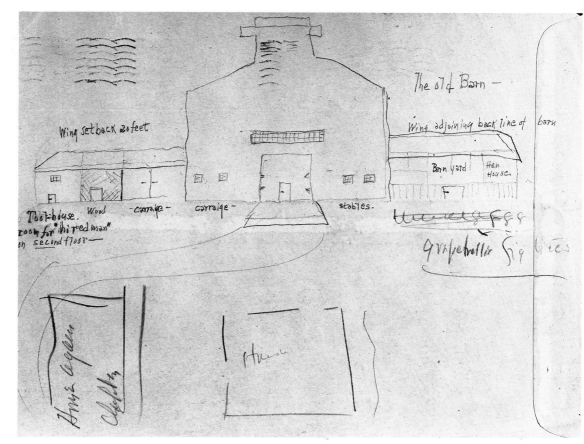

Opposite above. Emily Dickinson welcomed her
sister-in-law into the family with a poem.

Opposite below. A new home, named the
Evergreens by Sue and Austin, was built for the
newlyweds by Edward Dickinson west of the
homestead. Both houses are visible in this Lovell
view from the west on Main Street, n.d.

Sue Gilbert and Austin Dickinson were married
1 July 1856 in Geneva, New York, at the home of
the William Van Vrankens, the bride's aunt and
uncle. Both daguerreotypes ca. 1856.

Austin contemplated going west to set up practice, but
his father induced him to stay in Amherst. From *The
Hampshire and Franklin Express*.

Law Partnership.

THE undersigned have associated themselves
as Attorneys and Counsellors at Law, under the name of E. & A. Dickinson.

EDWARD DICKINSON,
W. AUSTIN DICKINSON.

Amherst, Oct. 31, 1855.   tf10

One Sister have I in our house,
And one, a hedge away.
There's only one recorded,
But both belong to me.

One came the road that I came —
And wore my last year's gown —
The other, as a bird her nest,
Builded our hearts among.

She did not sing as we did —
It was a different tune —
Herself to her a music
As Bumble bee of June.

Today is far from Childhood —
But up and down the hills
I held her hand the tighter —
Which shortened all the miles —

And still her hum
The years among,
Deceives the Butterfly;
Still in her Eye
The Violets lie
Mouldered this many May.

I spilt the dew —
But took the morn —
I chose this single star
From out the wide night's numbers —
Sue — forevermore!

Emilie.

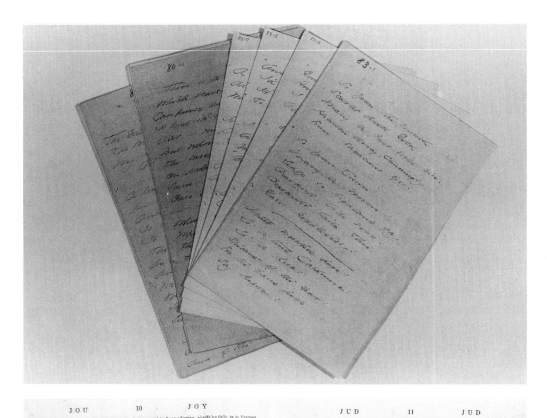

In December 1857 Ralph Waldo Emerson lectured at the village church and spent the night at the Evergreens. There is no record of whether Emily Dickinson heard or spoke with him.

Treasured Dickinson books were *Jane Eyre* and *Wuthering Heights* by Charlotte and Emily Brontë, respectively, and Emerson's *Poems,* given her by Benjamin Franklin Newton, her father's law student, who before his early death encouraged her to write poetry.

Opposite above. About 1858, perhaps to create order among her manuscripts, Dickinson began copying finished poems into small booklets, or "fascicles," constructed by stacking and threading several sheets of folded notepaper. *Left to right:* fascicles 1, 2, and 5. Number 5 is untied and fanned into its four folded sheets.

Opposite below. "For several years, my Lexicon—was my only companion—" the poet wrote editor Thomas Wentworth Higginson, of her apprentice period. Her two-volume dictionary opened here to leaves between which she pressed a clover, was the 1841 edition of *Webster's American Dictionary of the English Language* published at Amherst in 1844 by J. S. and C. Adams.

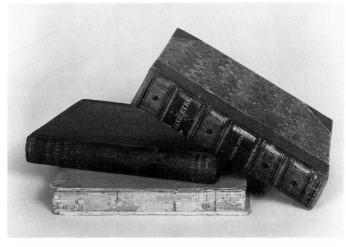

By 1858 College Row finally resembled this lithograph, first prepared for the trustees in 1828 and published several times before Appleton Cabinet, *right,* and Williston Hall, *left,* were built in 1855 and 1858, respectively.

Right. William Augustus Stearns became the fourth president of Amherst, 1854–1876.

Left. Amherst President Edward Hitchcock saw the college through its bleakest financial period, 1845–1854.

Edward Dickinson's solution to his daughter's fear of going into public alone was a large Newfoundland. Emily Dickinson named the dog Carlo, and her "shaggy ally" accompanied her on calls and walks for fifteen years. This road leading north out of Amherst, photographed by J. L. Lovell in 1861, shows the countryside they sometimes explored.

Local men outside the Field building on Amity Street in 1859, with Dr. Field in his wagon. Standing by the back wheel is Austin Dickinson.

View of Amherst looking north by John Bachelder, Endicott
& Co., New York, 1858, from an ambrotype by E.W. Cowles.

1860–1870

In the early 1860s Emily Dickinson endured an unexplained emotional crisis so wrenching that poems poured from her pen, as if she were writing for her life. It was a time of national chaos and also a period during which she suffered a problem with her vision of sufficient seriousness that she may have feared losing her eyesight. The predominant themes of love, loss, and grief among the poems of fascicles 8–19 convey a sense of heartbreak, though whom Dickinson may have loved has never been determined.

During these years she established a literary relationship with Boston writer and editor Thomas Wentworth Higginson, whom she asked to be her "preceptor." In seeking his "surgery" on mature poems whose astonishing psychological insights and unorthodox verbal strategies bewildered Higginson, she seems more probably to have needed his backing for her determination to defer publishing. Although she shared copies of her poems with select friends, she guarded against any escaping into print. Still, several poems appeared anonymously during the 1860s.

Opposite above. Looking north from the tower of Amherst College's Johnson Chapel in the mid-1860s. Despite efforts to fill, grade, and fence the common, the frog pond in its center was still apparent.

Opposite below. Amherst College from the west in the mid-1860s.

Merchants' Row in the early 1860s, when the Post Office occupied the white brick building on the right. Two doors further left
is the bookshop of J. S. and C. Adams, the literary center of the
village, where many volumes in the Dickinson library were pur-
chased. In the leftmost building is the general store of William
and George Cutler, with a crowd out front.

Opposite above. Looking west up Main Street in the early
1860s, past the lower end of Phoenix Row *(right)* to the
Amherst House at the village's main intersection. This was
the Dickinsons' view as they walked to the village center
from the homestead.

Opposite below. Looking east down Main Street along Phoenix Row, from the steps of the Amherst House, 1866.

Good friends of Dickinson's by 1860 were Josiah Gilbert Holland, cultural editor of the *Springfield Republican,* later editor of *Scribner's Monthly,* and his wife Elizabeth, whom the poet called Sister. Over the years Dickinson sent Mrs. Holland nearly one hundred letters and poems.

Left. Catharine Scott Turner (later Anthon) was a friend of Sue Dickinson's and a visitor to the Evergreens whom Emily liked enormously.

Right. Maria Whitney of Northampton, a favorite of all the Dickinsons. Her devotion to Samuel Bowles, to whose wife she was related, provided a quiet drama that engaged Dickinson's empathy. Miss Whitney's bond with Bowles seems to have remained a friendship.

Samuel Bowles, editor of New England's most influential newspaper, *The Springfield Republican,* trustee of Amherst College, and the Dickinsons' close friend. The poet's correspondence with him began in 1858; he dubbed her the "Queen Recluse."

Mary Schermerhorn Bowles was less adept socially than her prominent husband. She kept close to home tending their large family.

The third of ten poems known to have been published during Dickinson's lifetime. Under the title "The May-Wine" it appeared anonymously in the morning and evening editions of *The Springfield Republican* on 4 May 1861 and was reprinted in the *Springfield Weekly Republican* on 11 May 1861. The photograph here was taken from the poet's fair copy in fascicle 12. Her habit of marginal revision is evident; pencil markings at top are by subsequent editors.

Girlhood playmate Helen Fiske, *above,* and her husband, Major Edward B. Hunt's annual, *right,* attended the Dickinson's commencement tea on the homestead lawn in August 1860. According to editor Thomas Wentworth Higginson, the poet told him years later that "Major Hunt interested her more than any man she ever saw."

Above. Two liberal ministers who interested Emily
Dickinson were John Langdon Dudley, *left,* of Middletown,
Connecticut, who married her friend and second cousin
Eliza Coleman; and Rev. Charles Wadsworth, *right,* of Phil-
adelphia, whose departure in the spring of 1862 for a San
Francisco pulpit may have been traumatic for Dickinson.

Left. This undated note from Sue Dickinson to her sister-in-
law next door could be a clue to the "terror- since September"
that Dickinson endured in the autumn of 1861, or key to
the chaotic but unidentified event with which many
poems and letters of 1862 are concerned. The note has
been scissored into thirds.

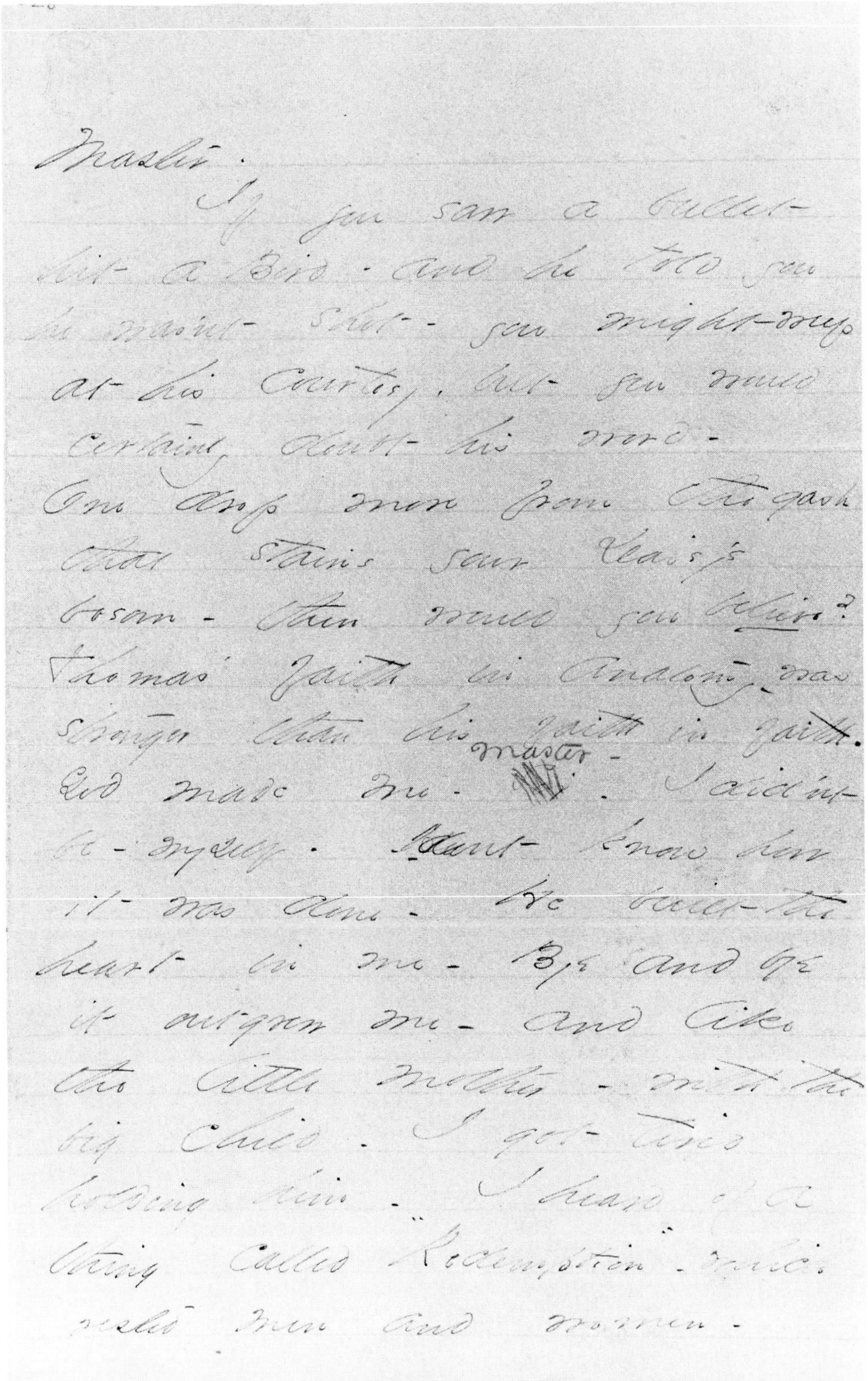

Master.
If you saw a bullet
hit a Bird - and he told you
he was'nt shot - you might weep
at his courtesy, but you would
certainly doubt his word -
One drop more from the gash
that stains your Daisy's
bosom - then would you believe?
Thomas' faith in Anatomy, was
stronger than his faith in faith.
God made me - Master - I did'nt
be - myself. I dont know how
it was done - He built the
heart in me - Bye and bye
it outgrew me - and like
the little mother - with the
big child - I got tired
holding him - I heard of a
thing called "Redemption" - which
rested men and women -

Beginning of a seven-page letter to "Master," the third of three extant drafts written to an unidentified correspondent between spring 1858 and summer 1861. That Dickinson loved but was not loved in return seems unmistakable from these much-revised manuscripts that survived among her poems.

Samuel Bowles's vibrant personality, particularly his "knack of drawing out plain and unattractive people," made him a popular visitor to Dr. E. E. Denniston's water cure in Northampton during the fall of 1861 when he suffered from sciatica. Dickinson turned to him for solace in her personal crisis at the time. *Below*, one of about a dozen letters and poems she sent him in late 1861 and early 1862.

Two Dickinson poems on typical themes. "Safe in their Alabaster Chambers," *above,* went through several drafts while Emily sought Sue's opinion in 1861. An early version appeared anonymously in the *Springfield Daily Republican* on 1 March 1862 under the title "The Sleeping." This fair copy is in fascicle 10.

"The face I carry with me- last-," *right,* is a "Master" poem, written ca. 1862. Dickinson initially intended to send it to someone (traces remain of folds and an erased name on the verso), but instead placed it at the end of fascicle 19.

Dickinson approached writer and editor Reverend Thomas Wentworth Higginson after reading his article "Letter to a Young Contributor" in the April 1862 issue of *The Atlantic Monthly.* Her letter, *below,* began their life-long correspondence. In place of a signature, Dickinson enclosed her handwritten calling card, along with four poems.

Mr Higginson,

Are you too deeply occupied to say if my Verse is alive?

The Mind is so near itself - it cannot see, distinctly - and I have none to ask -

Should you think it breathed - and had you the leisure to tell me, I should feel quick gratitude -

If I make the mistake - that you dared to tell me - would give me sincerer honor - toward you -

I enclose my name - asking you, if you please - Sir - to tell me what is true?

That you will not betray me - it is needless to ask - since Honor is its own pawn -

Above. The Civil War death at the Battle of New Bern of Frazar Stearns, *left,* one of Amherst's favorite youths, was a sorrow shared by many in the village, including Emily Dickinson. *Above right:* William S. Clark of the 21st Massachusetts Volunteers, Frazar's Amherst College chemistry professor and his commanding officer, near whom he fell.

Right. This six-pounder brass cannon captured by the 21st Massachusetts Regiment at New Bern was presented to the regiment by General Burnside in Frazar Stearns's memory and forwarded to his family in Amherst.

Perez Dickinson Cowan, the poet's favorite "Cousin Peter," was the grandson of Samuel Fowler Dickinson's brother Perez. He came to Amherst College in 1863 from Tennessee when his Uncle Perez Dickinson fled north through Confederate lines.

In 1864 Reverend Richard Salter Storrs solicited three Dickinson poems for *Drum Beat,* the daily newspaper he edited during the two-week Brooklyn Sanitary Fair, a Civil War fund-raising effort. Storrs, who had connections with the New York *Independent* and the *Brooklyn Daily Union,* was minister of the Church of the Pilgrims in Brooklyn. The Storrs and the Dickinson families had many ties through three generations.

Somebody who knows, says that when two or more women, approaching you on a narrow walk, fall behind one another to enable you to pass, you may be sure they are ladies of uncommon politeness and consideration. The usual course pursued by women is to charge all abreast, sweeping everybody into the mud.

Praise is not worth much, and I always take care when I am its object to receive it as a pleasant sensation, as metal which has not been assayed, and, if I do not use caution, as very probably a source of injury. Praise should always be considered a free-will offering rather than as a deserved reward.—*German writer.*

A West Indian, who had a remarkably red nose, having fallen asleep in his chair, a negro boy who was in waiting observed a mosquito hovering round his face. Quashy eyed it very attentively; at last it lit upon his master's nose, and instantly flew off again. "Yah, yah," he exclaimed with great glee, "me berry glad to see you burn your fut."

SUNSET.

Blazing in gold, and quenching in purple,
  Leaping like leopards in the sky,
Then at the feet of the old horizon
  Laying her spotted face to die;
Stooping as low as the oriel window,
  Touching the roof, and tinting the barn,
Kissing her bonnet to the meadow—
  And the Juggler of Day is gone!

A soldier in the Armory square hospital, Wash-

Storrs published Dickinson's poem "Sunset" among other anonymous contributions by popular writers in *Drum Beat*'s 29 February 1864 issue. It was subsequently picked up by the *Springfield Daily Republican* on 30 March and printed again in the "Wit and Wisdom" column of the *Springfield Weekly Republican* on 2 April. This reproduction is from the third-named source.

Charles Sweetser, nephew of Dickinson's neighbor Luke Sweetser, grew up in his uncle's Amherst home. His meteoric career in journalism, ended at age thirty by tuberculosis, included founding a New York literary weekly, *The Round Table,* in which he published Dickinson's poem "My Sabbath" on 12 March 1864.

One of three known copies of Dickinson's "Sabbath" poem, this was sent by the poet to Thomas Wentworth Higginson with three other poems in July 1862. The copy that found its way into *The Round Table* may be one now lost, given by Dickinson to Gordon Ford of Brooklyn.

Some keep the Sabbath
going to Church -
I keep it, staying at Home -
With a Bobolink for
a Chorister -
And an Orchard, for
a Dome -

Some keep the Sabbath
in Surplice -
I just wear my Wings -
And instead of tolling
the Bell . for Church,
Our little Sexton . sings.

God preaches, a
noted Clergyman -
And the sermon is
never long,
So instead of getting to
Heaven . at last -
I'm going, all along.

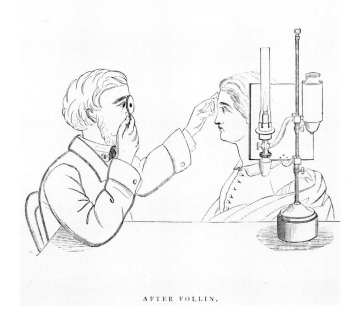

AFTER FOLLIN.

From April to November 1864 and again from April to November 1865, Emily Dickinson was treated by Boston's Dr. Henry Willard Williams for an undisclosed eye ailment. She resided both times in a Cambridgeport boarding house with her young cousins Louisa and Frances (Loo and Fanny) Norcross, to whom she was devoted. *Left,* the frontispiece of Dr. Williams's book, *Recent Advances in Ophthalmic Science,* 1866, depicts his diagnostic use of the ophthalmoscope and suggests the treatment Dickinson encountered.

Office appointments were held in Dr. Williams' new brown sandstone home opposite Boston's Public Garden, on the corner of Arlington and Newbury Streets, where the Ritz Carlton Hotel stands today. Photograph by Josiah Johnson Hawes, late 1860s.

Déposé. Registered.

24 R. Lehmann
BROWNING-BARRETT

Verlagsanstalt F. Bruckmann A.-G. in München.

The lives as well as the writings of Elizabeth Barrett-Browning and George Eliot fascinated Dickinson. She wrote three poems in tribute to Mrs. Browning after the latter's death in 1861 and kept portraits of both women on her bedroom wall.

Above. Elizabeth Barrett-Browning was "that Foreign Lady," and "the Anglo-Florentine" to Dickinson.

Right. "God chooses repellant settings, dont he, for his best Gems?" wrote Dickinson to Mrs. Holland about George Eliot's portrait.

Susan Dickinson was now a busy mother and a skilled hostess, as well as Emily Dickinson's first critic. By 1865 Emily Dickinson had shared over one hundred poems with her.

Sue and Austin's son Ned, here age 10, was born 19 June 1861.

Martha Dickinson (Mattie) was born 29 November 1866.

The Evergreens, where prominent guests enjoyed the Austin Dickinson's hospitality, especially during Amherst College trustee meetings and commencement. Photograph by Charles Prouty, ca. 1870.

Left. The Evergreens parlor in the nineteenth century. Sue Dickinson was noted for her taste and for the charm of her home.

The path between the two Dickinson homes, used by members of the family many times a day. View is to the west, toward the Evergreens. Austin Dickinson's pleasure in landscaping is apparent.

Right. The Dickinson homestead on Main Street. At upper left, the two south windows of the poet's bedroom.

Opposite right. A corner of the Evergreens dining room early in the twentieth century, after furnishings from the homestead had been incorporated into the decor.

In the 1930s, after the homestead was sold out of the family, Martha Dickinson Bianchi created a "Dickinson Room" at the Evergreens to display belongings of her Aunt Emily. Notable here are a corner of the poet's cherry bureau and the painted Hitchcock-style chair and small cherry writing table she used in her bedroom. These objects are now in the Dickinson Room of the Houghton Library at Harvard University.

A lone survivor of the exclusively white dresses Dickinson is known to have worn after the mid-1860s. Because of her reticence, dressmakers fitted the poet's garments to Lavinia Dickinson, who was about the same size.

Emily Dickinson's conservatory, off the homestead's dining room, where she coaxed exotic plants and blooms through the winter months. Her second writing table stood in a corner of the dining room, at the window shaded by honeysuckle. Photograph by Lincoln Barnes, ca. 1916.

The large Dickinson meadow across
from the homestead. The sounds and
scents of rowan being mowed were bliss-
ful summer occurrences for the poet.
Picture from the 1880s.

Lavinia Dickinson in the 1860s.
Practical, sociable, a superb
mimic, Vinnie acted as protectress
of the brilliant sister of whom she
was so proud.

The new First Congregational Church, built in 1868 on Main Street. View from the Evergreen's front gate, by George M. Lovell, 1869.

Reverend Jonathan L. Jenkins, much-loved pastor of the First Congregational Church from 1867 to 1877, with his children Sally ("Did") and MacGregor ("Mac"). These children, along with Ned and Mattie Dickinson, are the ones to whom the poet lowered gingerbread in a basket from her bedroom window. After leaving Amherst, Mr. Jenkins always returned to conduct Dickinson family funerals. Photograph by J. L. Lovell. *Right:* Mrs. Sara Eaton Jenkins.

In 1865, after passage of the Morrill Act, Amherst became the site of The Massachusetts Agricultural College, whose buildings added new interest to the area just north of the town center. The Durfee Plant House, built between 1867 and 1868, became a popular excursion point.

Winter view of Amherst, looking north from the new Grace Episcopal Church just after the tower was built in 1868.

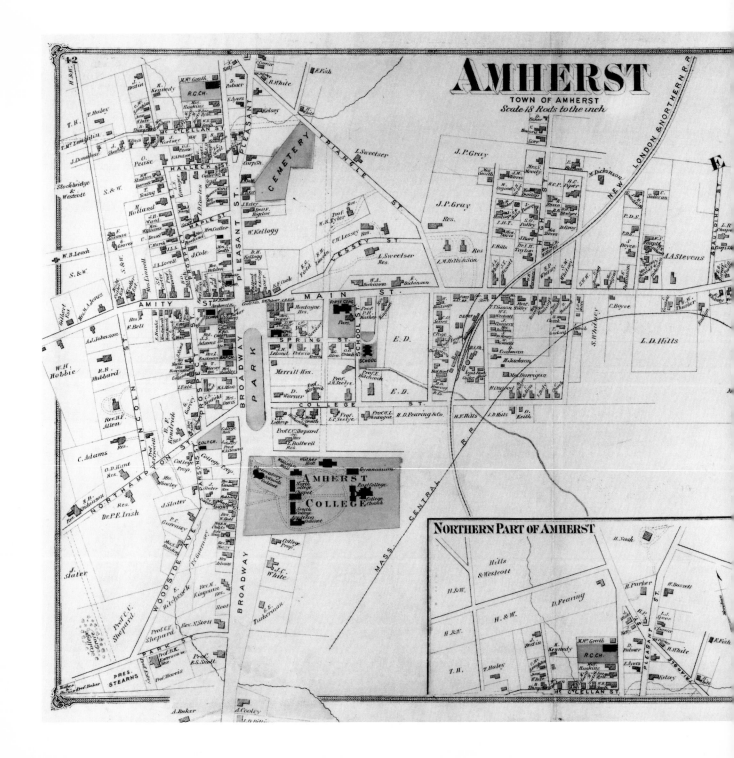

AMHERST
TOWN OF AMHERST
Scale 18 Rods to the inch

42

NORTHERN PART OF AMHERST

AMHERST COLLEGE

CEMETERY

PARK

1870–1886

Amherst 43

Business Notices

Colleges
Stearns W. A...Prest, Amherst College
Dickinson E...Treas, "
Crowell E. P..Prof, "
Emerson B. K.. "
Hitchcock E... "
Mather R. H.. "
Shepard C. U.. "
Snell E. S... "
Tyler W. S... "
Clark W. S..Prest, Mass. Agricultural College
Goodell H..Prof, "
Peabody E. H.. "
Stockbridge L.. "

Attorneys
Dickinson E..Atty. at Law, Palmer's Block
Dickinson S... "
Dickinson W. A..Atty. at Law, Palmer's Block
Turkerman G. E.. " Phoenix Row
Ward H... "

Books and Stationery
Adams J. S. & C..Dealers in Books, Stationery, &c.,
Broadway

Carpenter and Builder
Lessey C. W...Contractor and Builder, Lessey St

Dry and Fancy Goods
Kellogg Wm...Dealer in Dry and Fancy Goods, &c.,
Phoenix Row
Pease O..Dealer in Dry and Fancy Goods, &c., Broad-
way

Druggist
Deuel Chas..Dealer in Drugs, Medicines, &c., Phoenix
Row

Dentist
Vincent J. J...Dentist, Palmer's Block

Hotel
Amherst House..Geo. E. Parker, Propr

Jeweler
Parker G. L...Dealer in Watches, Clocks, Jewelry, &c.,
Amity cor. Pleasant

Manufacturer
Hills L. D...Importer of Palm Leaf and Manufacturer
of Palm Leaf Goods, Main St., near Depot

Physicians
Bigelow O. F..Physician and Surgeon, Pleasant St.,
near Maple
Irish F. E..Physician and Surgeon, Northampton St
Taylor I. H..Physician and Surgeon, High St., near
Main

Stoves and Tinware
Hunt O. D..Dealer in Stoves, Tinware, &c., Broadway

Miscellaneous
Mt. Pleasant Institute..H. Nash, Principal, Pleasant
St
Allen Rev. H. F...Rector Episcopal Church, Pleasant St
Jenkins Rev. R. L...Pastor Congregational Church
Brennan F..Parish Priest, R. C. Church

Adams A...Farmer	Hobbs W. H..Farmer
Adams C... "	Hills L. M.. "
Baker J... "	Hubbard R. B.. "
Baker A... "	Kellogg S... "
Baker C. A.. "	King Amos... "
Bassett A... "	King E. A.. "
Belden B... "	King A... "
Billings J. D.. "	Lovett E... "
Boltwood E.. "	McMaster C.. "
Cooley A... "	Nunnell G. G.. "
Cook H... "	Newell G. W.. "
Chapin G. H.. "	Potwin J. J.. "
Churchill J. W..Farmer	Prince G... "
Dickinson S... "	Richardson H. B.. "
Dickinson C.. "	Stanley E. A.. "
Dickinson M. B.. "	Stevens A. A.. "
Dexter D... "	Stocking W.. "
Drigg J... "	Sweetser L... "
Fearing D... "	Taylor H... "
Fish E... "	Woods R. M.. "
Gaylord F... "	White C... "
Granger L. N.. "	White J. C.. "
Gray J. F... "	Whitney E. P.. "
Harlow N. L.. "	Whitney S. W.. "

The 1873 Beers Atlas is a detailed, ambitious map of the village. Attempts to upgrade the common to a park and to change the name of South Pleasant Street to Broadway went unrealized. The route of the Massachusetts Central Railroad, which L. M. Hills hoped would bend through his hat factory, took a straighter east–west course south of town when it was finally built in 1887.

By 1870 Amherst was a bustling community of 4,035 residents, not including the students at Amherst College and the Massachusetts Agricultural College. Although Emily Dickinson was fully reclusive by this time ("I do not cross my Father's ground to any House or town"), her father's and brother's involvement in every important legal and civic activity in the village kept her knowledgable of all that went on. Her intensive correspondences with friends and the many attentions of food and flowers she sent to neighbors attest to her involvement in the lives around her.

In the late 1870s Emily Dickinson fell in love with Judge Otis Phillips Lord of Salem. Eighteen years her senior, Lord was a judge of the Massachusetts Superior Court, and a widower. As an Amherst College graduate (1832) and her father's close friend, he had often been, with his wife, in Dickinson's home. Now he began to correspond with and occasionally visit Emily to press his suit. From extant drafts of letters to Judge Lord among her surviving papers, it is clear the poet considered marriage, a step forestalled, if not by her own hesitations, by Lord's stroke in 1882 and his death in 1884.

The deaths of many persons she loved—her parents, Samuel Bowles, Judge Lord, and others—filled the last dozen years of Dickinson's life and give to her late poems an air of elegy. Dickinson herself succumbed to Bright's disease on 15 May 1886 after more than two years of intermittent illness.

Opposite above. This view northwest from the Amherst College tower in 1870 shows the octagonal observatory and the natural history cabinet, *foreground. Middle, from left to right:* College president's house, Morgan Library, and College Hall (the former village church, without its portico).

Opposite below. Looking northeast from the college tower in 1871, the foreground is occupied by Walker Hall, the new "Temple of Science and Mathematics." In the distance, *left,* the public high school; *center background,* the wide, open Dickinson meadow; to right of Walker Hall roof, the Hills Hat Factory. Beyond are the homes of Amherst's swelling population of factory and construction workers.

The Amherst House, the village's central hotel, early spring 1872. Behind it, on the former site of the Amherst Academy, stands the Amity Street Public School, built in 1868.

Opposite above. Merchants' Row, from the Amherst common, early spring 1869. William and George Cutler's general store, with shovels on porch, was well patronized by both Dickinson families.

Opposite below. A view up North Pleasant Street, 1866, with sign for O. D. Hunt's stove and tinware shop, *right*.

929

Commonwealth of Massachusetts.
House of Representatives.
Boston, June 5ᵗʰ 1874

[handwritten letter, Edward Dickinson, signature E. Dickinson]

[handwritten elegy, Emily Dickinson]

Above. Edward Dickinson's last letter to Austin, written from Boston, where he was serving a term in the General Court to try to hasten construction of the Massachusetts Central Railroad. He died at his boarding house on 15 June 1874 after faltering at the State House during a speech on the Hoosac Tunnel Bill.

Left. Emily Dickinson's elegy to her father was sent to Thomas Wentworth Higginson on the third anniversary of Edward Dickinson's death, in June 1877.

Edward Dickinson, in the only extant likeness, 1853. Stores
closed in Amherst the day of his funeral.

Austin Dickinson, ca. 1870. Austin succeeded his father as Amherst College treasurer and came into his own as the town's indispensable man.

Reverend Julius H. Seelye became president of Amherst College in 1877, having been professor of Mental and Moral Philosophy at the college since 1858. He and Austin Dickinson were excellent friends.

For many decades the Dickinson law office was housed on the second foor, *left corner,* of the Palmer Block. Today Amherst's town hall occupies the site. *On right,* the home of James Cooper, Austin Dickinson's law partner from 1878 to 1895.

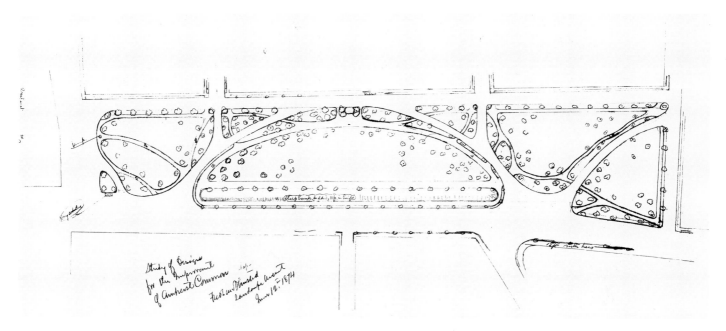

Frederick Law Olmsted's plan for beautifying the town common, designed at the request of Austin Dickinson, 1874.

The Amherst common as it appeared about 1870. Though Olmsted's plan was never realized, the appearance of the common improved considerably after it was drawn.

Samuel Bowles died in early 1878 at fifty-one, causing great grief among his friends. "That he has received Immortality who so often conferred it, invests it with a more sudden charm," Emily Dickinson wrote to Maria Whitney in Northampton.

By the mid-1870s Dickinson had sent Thomas Wentworth Higginson (shown here with daughter Margaret, ca. 1884) over fifty poems. In November 1875, Higginson read some of them anonymously to the New England Women's Club of Boston during a talk on "Two unknown Poetesses." "Their weird & strange power excited much interest," he reported. By then he had called twice on the poet at the homestead, in 1870 and 1873.

Opposite above. Dickinson's acquaintance with Helen Hunt Jackson, *left, facing camera,* one of the period's popular authors, was renewed when "H.H." begged the Amherst poet to let her include "Success" in the anonymous volume *A Masque of Poets,* published in 1878 by Roberts Brothers of Boston. The poem, *right,* appeared, apparently without permission, and was attributed by critics to Emerson.

Opposite below. During the last decade of their lives Helen Hunt Jackson and Emily Dickinson exchanged about a dozen extant letters and as many poems. About 1879 Dickinson pencilled H.H. a copy of her poem on the hummingbird.

SUCCESS.

SUCCESS is counted sweetest
By those who ne'er succeed.
To comprehend a Nectar
Requires the sorest need.
Not one of all the Purple Host
Who took the flag to-day,
Can tell the definition,
So plain, of Victory,
As he defeated, dying,
On whose forbidden ear
The distant strains of triumph
Break, agonizing clear.

Dear friend,
    To the Oriole
you suggested
I add a Humming
Bird and hope
they are not untrue.

A Route of
Evanescence
With a revolving
Wheel
A Resonance of
Emerald
A Rush of
Cochineal

And every
Blossom on the
Bush
Adjusts it's
tumbled Head -
The mail from
Tunis, probably,
An easy morning's
Ride.

171

Amherst September 1893

Merchandise forward   297.60

#329 Edward Dickinson   82

6	20	Pa C Starch			14·	
8		1 c Cocoanut			45.	
9		6 c Graham	6	36		
		Gran Sugar		200	2.36	
18		1 Gal Kerosene			35.	
20		1 c Ginger Snaps		20		
		½ Gal Molasses	80	40	.60·	
23		2 c Sweet Potatoes	6		12.	
30		1 c Ginger Snaps			20.	4.22

#190 W. A. Dickinson   80

1	20	2 Boys Wb Shirts	112	224		
		½ Yd Lace	40	20		
		1¾ Merino	138	242	4.86·	
2		3 c Gran Sugar	9		38·	
3		Pr Lacets			02·	
24		1 yd Blk cord dld. self			13·	
30		2 Gals Kerosene	35	70		
		6 c Sweet Potatoes	6	36	1.06	6.45

Left. Page from the account ledger at William and George Cutler's general store showing purchases by the two Dickinson families.

Opposite below left. Margaret (Maggie) Maher, *left,* worked in the Dickinson household thirty years, beginning in 1869; her one-armed brother-in-law, Thomas Kelley, worked on the Dickinson properties, and was chief pallbearer at the poet's funeral; Margaret Kelley, Tom Kelley's daughter, worked for the Austin Dickinsons at the Evergreens. Photograph ca. 1870.

Opposite below right. Pencilled draft for a poem Dickinson wrote in the mid-1870s using a slit-open envelope as a worksheet. Dozens of her later poems survive on household scrap paper.

Left. Mattie Dickinson, age six.

Right. Ned Dickinson, on his thirteen birthday.

Left. Mrs. Holland, ca. 1880, still Emily Dickinson's great friend.

Right. Thomas Gilbert Dickinson ("Gib"), born to Sue and Austin in 1875.

Judge Otis Phillips Lord, of Salem. He and Emily
Dickinson fell in love in the late 1870s.

Part of a drafted love letter to Judge Lord found among
Dickinson's papers after her death.

Opposite above. Fire devastated Merchants Row the
night of 3 July 1879. "I could hear buildings falling, and
oil exploding," Dickinson wrote to Loo and Fanny Norcross. The worst of many fires Amherst suffered through
the years, this one prompted the village to build a public
water system supplied by a Pelham reservoir. The buildings on Merchants' Row, including the Amherst House
and Cutler's general store, where the fire began, were
rebuilt with insurance money.

Opposite below. The common on 4 July 1879, littered
with what could be pulled from the flames. *Right:*
Amherst's single hook-and-ladder engine.

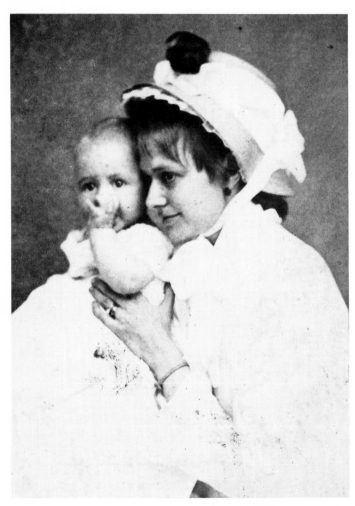

In September 1881 David Peck Todd (*below right,* in 1882), a graduate of Amherst College, returned to teach astronomy and mathematics. He was accompanied by his talented wife, Mabel Loomis Todd of Washington, D.C., posed here with their six-month-old daughter Millicent, 1880.

Although Mabel Todd never saw Emily Dickinson while the poet lived, she was often invited to the homestead to play the piano for Emily and for the bedridden Mrs. Dickinson. Photograph from Mme. Bianchi's Dickinson Room at the Evergreens, ca. late 1930s. Piano is now at the Houghton Library, Harvard University.

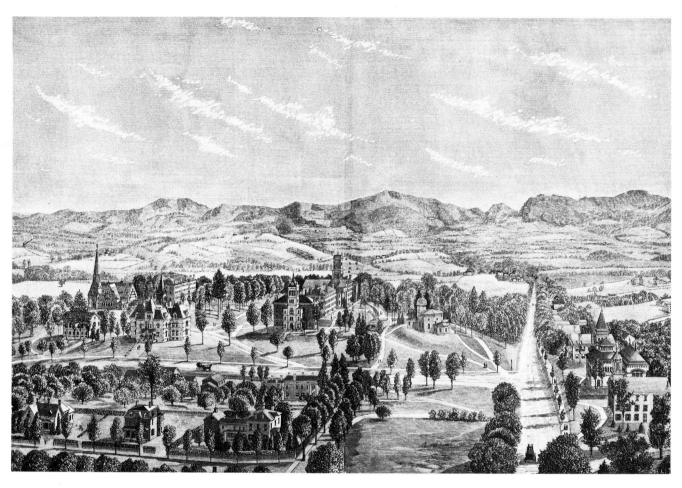

Amherst, viewed to the south from the center of town, from
L. H. Evert's *History of the Connecticut Valley in Massachusetts,* 1879.

Sue Dickinson's enter-
tainments were elabo-
rate. Here, the
Amherst stage, loaded
with picnickers en
route to spend the day
with Sue's camping
party in Shutesbury,
July 1882.

Members of Sue's camp-
ing trip dubbed them-
selves "The Shutesbury
School of Philosophy"
when they posed, upon
their return, at Mr.
Lovell's studio. Mabel
Loomis Todd is at rear
in wide-brimmed hat;
Sue Dickinson with
arms around Gib; Mattie
Dickinson in straw hat
near mantle; Ned
Dickinson lying front
right with tennis racket;
and David Todd
crouched behind Ned, in
straw bowler.

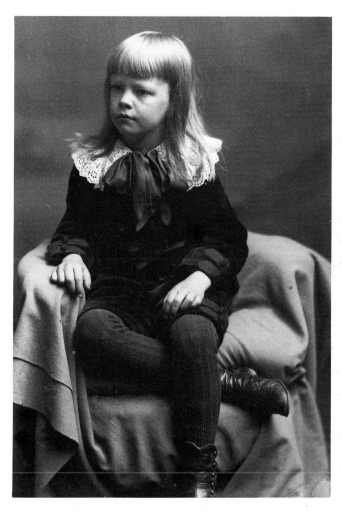

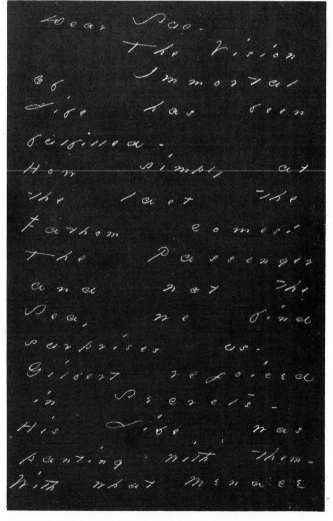

Above left. Gib, about six years old. In early October 1883 he died of typhoid, at age eight.

Above right. Children at Mrs. Howland's school, in her octagonal house on North Prospect Street, ca. 1883. Gib Dickinson stands in second row, *center,* in plaid suit with white collar.

Right. First page of a letter the grief-stricken Emily Dickinson sent to her sister-in-law.

Mabel Loomis Todd, March 1883. By September 1882, she and Austin Dickinson had fallen in love.

Mabel Todd's journal entry for 11 September 1882, the evening she and Mr. Dickinson first acknowledged their mutual feelings, bears only a series of dashes to suggest what could not be entrusted to writing. Pencilled *Rubicon* at bottom was entered later.

Austin Dickinson in the 1880s.

Right. The word *Rubicon* in Austin Dickinson's diary is the clue that he confessed his passion to Mrs. Todd as he escorted her to the Evergreens for an evening of whist.

This note, carried for twelve years in Austin Dickinson's wallet, signified the consummation of the love affair. Alternate letters spell their names. The same word occurs on a slip of paper dated 13 December 1883 and tucked into Mrs. Todd's diary at the page for that day.

Helen Hunt Jackson a few months before her death in San Francisco in August 1885. She had recently asked Dickinson to "make me your literary legatee & executor."

At the first gravesite for Helen Hunt Jackson on Cheyenne Mountain, Colorado Springs, Colorado, every visitor added a stone. She was later reburied in the town cemetery.

The death of the Rev. Charles Wadsworth in
April 1882 ended a friendship and correspondence dear to Dickinson. He had twice called
on her in Amherst, at twenty-year intervals. In
November of the same year, the bedridden Mrs.
Dickinson died. Her daughters had nursed her
for seven years.

Judge Otis Lord's death in
March 1884 was a severe
blow to Emily Dickinson.

Above left. Dr. O. F. Bigelow was Emily Dickinson's physician through the 2½ years of illness with Bright's disease that preceded her death on 15 May 1886.

Above right. On the day in 1875 that Mrs. Edward Dickinson had made her will, Emily did the same, using the same witnesses, among them Mrs. Otis Phillips Lord, who died in 1877.

Left. A page from the record book of Mr. Edwin Marsh, funeral director and cemetery superintendent, specifying the arrangements for Dickinson's funeral. Lavinia's tombstone stands today on the site marked here for Emily's grave.

Dickinson's casket was borne out the back door of the homestead (pictured here ca. 1916, before present-day portico was added) and carried cross-lots to the graveyard on a special bier on 19 May 1886.

The original gravestones in the fenced Dickinson plot. The poet's, in the center, bore just her initials, *E.E.D.*

The Dickinson gravestones were replaced in the twentieth century by Martha Dickinson Bianchi. *From left to right:* Lavinia, Emily, Mr. and Mrs. Edward Dickinson, and Mr. and Mrs. Samuel Fowler Dickinson. Emily Dickinson's tablet bears the message *Called Back.*

Part of a view of Amherst, published by Burleigh Lithographers, Troy, New York, 1886. View is toward the northwest, from the southeast corner of the village.

The Poets light but Lamps—
Themselves—go out—
The Wicks they stimulate—
If vital Light

Inhere as do the Suns—
Each Age a Lens
Disseminating their
Circumference—

—Emily Dickinson

The Dell, a Queen
Anne cottage built
by David and Mabel
Todd in 1886 on
land given them by
Austin Dickinson
when he cut a road
through the south
end of the Dickin-
son meadow.
(1887).

Mrs. Todd's parlors
in the Dell. The
upper friezes in
both rooms, the
standing screen,
mirror, and cup-
board door all dis-
play her artwork.

Mabel Loomis Todd, 1885, wearing dress with panels on which she painted sweetpeas.

Austin Dickinson in 1890. His love affair with Mabel Todd created great unhappiness within the Evergreens.

Amherst's Palmer Block burned the night of the Blizzard of
1888, 13 March, destroying Austin Dickinson's law office
and many old town records housed within.

The Dickinson homestead in 1886.

Emily Dickinson's cherry bureau, in which Lavinia found some of her sister's poems. Picture is from Martha Dickinson Bianchi's Dickinson Room at the Evergreens, late 1930s. The bureau is now at the Houghton Library, Harvard University.

Determined to see her sister's poems published, Lavinia turned first to Col. Thomas Wentworth Higginson, then to Sue Dickinson, then to Mabel Todd. Here, Vinnie with one of her numerous beloved cats, on the east porch of the homestead, 1896.

Late in 1887, at Lavinia Dickinson's request, Mabel Todd began copying and organizing Emily Dickinson's hundreds of poems. Part of the work was done on this slow, unsophisticated World typewriter.

In November 1889 Mrs. Todd persuaded Thomas Wentworth Higginson to lend his prestige to the project as coeditor. Together they selected the choicest poems for publication. They also added titles, chose among Dickinson's alternative readings, and "smoothed" some rhymes.

Thomas Niles, editor of Roberts Brothers of Boston. In the late spring of 1890, at Mrs. Todd's request, he agreed to publish a small edition of 116 Dickinson poems if Lavinia Dickinson would pay for the plates.

The dainty 5″ × 7″ boxed, white volume with gold and silver stamping was published 12 November 1890 and by March was in its sixth edition. The cover design of Indian Pipes was reproduced from a painting Mabel Todd had made for Emily Dickinson in 1882; the poet thanked her for "the preferred flower of life." Further volumes of poems appeared in 1891 and 1896. Mrs. Todd also edited Dickinson's letters in two volumes, pictured here, in 1894.

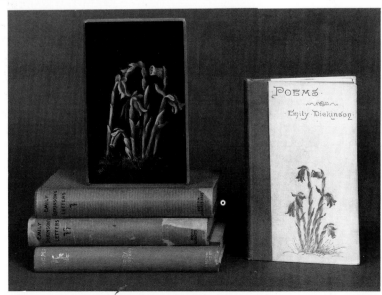

At Lavinia Dickinson's further urging in 1897, Laura Hills produced a ruff for Dickinson, shown here, *top,* partially developed. It satisfied the poet's sister. In 1924 Martha Dickinson Bianchi further retouched a photograph of Hills' finished ruff portrait and published it, *bottom,* in *The Life and Letters of Emily Dickinson.* Mrs. Todd republished her *Letters of Emily Dickinson* in 1931 using the original Dickinson daguerreotype for the first time. Bianchi's ruff portrait is still sometimes used to represent the poet, without explanation of its derivation.

Opposite Page: By 1893 the public was clamoring for a picture of Emily Dickinson. Family members disliked the daguerreotype, *upper left,* but attempts at that time to create a less severe likeness, *upper right; lower left,* seemed unpromising. In 1897 Boston miniaturist Laura C. Hills retouched for Lavinia the hair and neck of a photograph of the daguerreotype, *lower right,* and included a lace collar. None of these images was published, however. Instead, for her 1894 *Letters* Mrs. Todd isolated and used the child portrait of Emily by Bullard (see p. 17).

Right. The death of Austin Dickinson at sixty-six in August 1895 was a blow to the Amherst community. Sue Dickinson erected this plaque and boulder near his grave in Wildwood Cemetery, Amherst's new parklike burial ground that Austin had lovingly landscaped.

Below left. Within a year of Austin Dickinson's death, tensions between the Dickinsons and the Todds erupted into a lawsuit between Lavinia Dickinson and Mabel Todd over a piece of land claimed by both parties. Scandalous overtones made the court case a headline item by the time it came to trial in 1898.

Below right. Two weeks after the stressful trial ended with a verdict against Mrs. Todd, Ned Dickinson died of angina in May 1898, at the age of thirty-six.

HAMPSHIRE

NORTHAMPTON, MASS., THURSDAY, MARCH 3, 1898.

DICKINSON-TODD COURT CASE.

Miss Dickinson Says She Did Not Go Out in the Moonlight.

At the resumption of the Dickinson-Todd case today, Lawyer Spaulding took the stand. He testified to the conversation he had with Mrs. Todd about signing a deed and the request of Judge Bumpus of Boston, who wrote him asking that he attend to the business as Mrs. Todd was a personal friend of his. The letter was read and in speaking of Miss Dickinson Judge Bumpus referred to her as being a very sensitive woman and rather peculiar in some things. Mrs. Todd arranged with Mr. Spaulding to come to Amherst in the latter part of the afternoon. Mr. Spaulding said he went on a train that left Northampton about 5 o'clock. He first went to Mrs. Todd's house and then went to Miss Dickinson's house. Miss Dickinson came to the door. There was a conversation of nearly three quarters of an hour, during which various things were talked about before the subject of a deed was broached. Mrs. Todd had the deed and said it would be a good time to sign it. There would never be a better time to sign it.

Mr. Spaulding taking the deed said to Miss Dickinson, this appears to be a deed of land from you to Mrs. Todd. He read part of the deed when Miss Dickinson interrupted him by saying, "Yes, I understand all about it. We have talked it all over. But there is no hurry about signing it." Mr. Spaulding replied that as he was over in Amherst it was as good a time as it ever would be to sign it. Miss Dickinson replied, "Yes, I know that," and taking the deed went to her desk and signed it. Mr. Spaulding then witnessed her signature.

As Miss Dickinson signed the deed, she spoke of some furniture and china in the kitchen. Mr. Spaulding and Mrs. Todd remained about 15 minutes after the deed was signed.

After the signing Miss Dickinson spoke

Her sister Emily died on Dec. 16, 1886. She enjoyed good health and was able to attend to her household affairs, hire help, etc. She never had to discharge any servant, because they wanted to stay.

Margaret McMahon, who had worked in the Dickinson family 30 years, was called to testify in behalf of the plaintiff as to conversation that had taken place between Mrs. Todd and Miss Dickinson, but it was ruled out on objection of the defendant.

Court adjourned at noon and this afternoon arguments were made. Lawyer O'Donnell, who was called into the case by the defendant, in place of Judge Bassett, who had to leave Tuesday on account of probate business, made the plea for Mrs. Todd.

Last evening was the occasion of one of the most enjoyable whist parties yet given by the O. E. C. The club was entertained by one of its members and no pains were spared to make the event one not soon to be forgotten. This little club has been the source of much pleasure to its members the past winter.

Left. Following the trial Mabel Todd locked away the Dickinson materials in her possession, including over six hundred unpublished poems. Photograph taken in Japan, 1896.

Right. In 1945 Millicent Todd Bingham published the Dickinson poems her mother had held, and subsequently wrote three biographical studies of the Dickinson family as well. In 1956 Mrs. Bingham gave to Amherst College the Dickinson poems and Dickinson family papers she inherited from her mother. In 1968 she left her own and her parents' private papers to Yale University. She had no heirs. Photograph taken in 1905.

Left. Sue Dickinson lived on at the Evergreens, often traveling abroad with her daughter Martha. Here photographed in Berlin at age eighty.

Below right. After her mother's death, Martha Dickinson Bianchi brought out eight volumes of her Aunt Emily's poetry between 1914 and 1937. In 1950 the poems in her possession were sold, together with many family manuscripts and artifacts relating to Emily Dickinson, to an intermediary who gave them to Harvard University. Since Mme. Bianchi had no heirs, there are no direct descendants of Emily Dickinson. Photograph taken ca. 1910.

Gold-edged china
and a red and black
Towle tea tray used
in the Edward
Dickinson family.

Miss Emily E. Dickinson.

Emily Dickinson's calling card.

Characteristic of numerous "attentions" sent to friends and
neighbors is this Dickinson note that accompanied flowers
for Mrs. Timothy Sloan when her seventeen-year-old
daughter, Mary Emma, died in August 1883.

Emily Dickinson's watch, missing its hour hand, is displayed at the Houghton Library, Harvard University.

Emily Dickinson's brooch, in its case at the Houghton Library, Harvard University. It may be the same brooch Mrs. Dickinson wears in her daguerreotype, p. 41.

Two views of Dickinson's bedroom at the Dickinson homestead, Amherst, as it looks today. The house is owned by Amherst College and is maintained partially as a museum, open to the public certain weekdays by appointment.

REFERENCES AND CREDITS

References

All Emily Dickinson poems quoted and photographed within this book are reprinted by permission of the publishers and the Trustees of Amherst College from THE POEMS OF EMILY DICKINSON, Thomas H. Johnson, ed., Cambridge, MA: The Belknap Press of Harvard University Press, Copyright 1951 © 1955, 1979, 1983 by the President and Fellows of Harvard College.

All Emily Dickinson letters quoted and photographed within this book are reprinted by permission of the publishers from THE LETTERS OF EMILY DICKINSON, edited by Thomas H. Johnson, Cambridge, MA: The Belknap Press of Harvard University Press, Copyright © 1958, 1986 by the President and Fellows of Harvard College.

INTRODUCTION
p.1 "Could you believe me— . . ." ED to Thomas Wentworth Higginson, July 1862, *Letters,* vol. 2, no. 268.
p.1 "If fame belonged to me . . ." ED to Higginson, June 1862, *Letters* 2, no. 265.
p.2 "A village in the woods . . ." Prof. Charles Upham Shepard, quoted in William S. Tyler, *A History of Amherst College* (New York, 1895).
p.2 "The college buildings . . ." Thomas M. Howell, "Amherst Fifty Years Ago," *Amherst Record,* 27 July 1881.
p.3 "As the snow lay . . ." Susan Dickinson, "Annals of the Evergreens," published as "Two Generations of Society" in *Essays on Amherst's History,* ed. Theodore Greene (Amherst: Vista Trust, 1978).
p.3 "dreaming a *golden* dream" ED to Abiah Root, May 1850, *Letters* 1, no. 36.
p.3 "I know that Emily . . ." Louisa Norcross in a letter to *Woman's Journal,* 26 March 1904. See Gary Scharnhorst, "A Glimpse of Dickinson at Work," *American Literature* 57-3 (1985):484–85.
p.3 "too busy with . . ." ED to Higginson, April 1862, *Letters* 2, no. 261.
p.3 "does not care . . ." ED to Higginson, April 1862, *Letters* 2, no. 261.
p.3 "stares in a curious . . ." ED to Joseph Lyman, 1850s, *The Lyman Letters,* by Richard B. Sewall, (Amherst: University of Massachusetts Press, 1965), p. 70.
p.4 "You saved my Life," ED to Higginson, June 1869, *Letters* 2, no. 330.
p.4 "My friends are my . . ." ED to Samuel Bowles, late August 1858?, *Letters* 2, no. 193.
p.4 "They carried her . . ." Mabel Loomis Todd to her mother, 23 May 1886, quoted in Jay Leyda, *The Years and Hours of Emily Dickinson* (New Haven: Yale University Press, 1960), 2:474.
p.5 "The Poets light . . ." *Poems,* vol. 2, no. 883.

CAPTIONS
p.20 "No doubt you can . . ." ED to Austin Dickinson, July 1851, *Letters* 1, no. 46.
p.22 "There was always . . ." ED to Austin Dickinson, April 1842, *Letters* 1, no. 1.
p.25 "a very bright . . ." Daniel Taggart Fiske to Mabel Loomis Todd, quoted in Richard B. Sewall, *The Life of Emily Dickinson* (New York: Farrar, Straus & Giroux, 1974), 342.
p.27 "a fixed melancholy" ED to Abiah Root, March 1846, *Letters* 1, no. 11.
p.29 "The trees stand . . ." ED to Loo and Fanny Norcross, October 1863?, *Letters* 2, no. 286.
p.36 "I love this seminary . . ." ED to Abiah Root, January 1848, *Letters* 1, no. 20.
p.38 "carrying the Knives . . ." ED to Abiah Root, November 1847, *Letters* 1, no. 18.
p.47 *Herself* and not . . ." ED to Austin Dickinson, July 1851, *Letters* 1, no. 46.
p.53 "He was my . . ." ED to James D. Clark, August 1882, *Letters* 3, no. 766.
p.59 "For several years . . ." ED to Higginson, April 1862, *Letters* 2, no. 261.
p.70 "Major Hunt interested . . ." Higginson to Mrs. Higginson, August 1870, *Letters* 2, no. 342b.
p.71 "terror- since September" ED to Higginson, April 1862, *Letters* 2, no. 261.
p.73 "Knack of drawing . . ." A fellow patient with Bowles at Dr. Denniston's, quoted in Sewall, *Life,* 470.
p.80 "that Foreign Lady" *Poems* 2, no. 593.
p.80 "the Anglo-Florentine" *Poems* 1, no. 312.
p.80 "God chooses repellant . . ." ED to Mrs. Holland, Spring 1881, *Letters* 3, no. 692.
p.90 "I do not cross . . ." ED to Higginson, June 1869, *Letters* 2, no. 330.
p.98 "That he has . . ." ED to Maria Whitney, 1878, *Letters* 2, no. 537.
p.98 "Their weird & strange . . ." Higginson to his sister, November 1875, quoted in Leyda, *Years* 2:239.
p.103 "I could hear . . ." ED to Loo and Fanny Norcross, July 1879, *Letters* 2, no. 610.
p.110 "Make me your . . ." Helen Hunt Jackson to ED, September 1884, *Letters* 3, no. 937a.
p.116 "The Poets light but Lamps" *Poems* 2, no. 883.
p.123 "the preferred flower of life" ED to Mabel Loomis Todd, September 1882, *Letters* 3, no. 769.

Credits

p.ii Author's collection.

p.iii The Todd-Bingham Picture Collection, Yale University Library.

p.1 By permission of the Amherst Historical Society, Amherst, Massachusetts.

p.2 Courtesy of The Jones Library, Inc., Amherst, Massachusetts.

p.5 The Amherst College Archives.

p.7 Courtesy of The Jones Library, Inc., Amherst, Massachusetts.

p.8 *top:* By permission of the Houghton Library, Harvard University. *Bottom left:* Courtesy of Barton St. Armand, photograph by Richard Hurley; *bottom right:* Mead Art Museum, Amherst College, Gift of Arthur D. Norcross.

p.9 *Top:* Courtesy of Docia Jones Horton; *bottom left and right:* The Monson Free Library and Reading Room Association, Monson, Massachusetts.

p.10 *Top:* By permission of the Houghton Library, Harvard University; *bottom left and right:* Photographs from *The Life of Emily Dickinson* by Richard Sewall. Copyright © 1974, 1980 by Richard B. Sewall. Reprinted by permission of Farrar, Strauss & Giroux, Inc.

p.11 *Both:* Courtesy of The Jones Library, Inc., Amherst, Massachusetts.

p.12 *Top:* Courtesy of The Jones Library, Inc., Amherst, Massachusetts; *bottom:* The Amherst College Archives.

p.13 *Top:* Courtesy of William Woodward; *bottom:* The Todd-Bingham Picture Collection, Yale University Library.

p.14 *Top:* Yale Picture Collection, Yale University Library; *bottom left:* By permission of the Houghton Library, Harvard University; *bottom right:* Yale Class Albums, Yale University Library.

p.15 *Top:* The Monson Free Library and Reading Room Association, Monson, Massachusetts; *bottom left and right:* By permission of the Houghton Library, Harvard University.

p.16 *Top:* Courtesy of The Jones Library, Inc., Amherst, Massachusetts; *bottom:* Courtesy of The Dickinson Homestead, Amherst College; photograph by Frank Ward.

p.17 By permission of the Houghton Library, Harvard University.

p.18 The Amherst College Archives.

p.19 *Top:* Courtesy of the Board of Trustees of the Lane Seminary, Cincinnati, Ohio, and the Jesuit-Krauss-McCormick Library (Lane Archives), Chicago, Illinois; *Bottom:* Courtesy The Case Western Reserve University Archives.

p.20 *Top:* By permission of the Houghton Library, Harvard University; *bottom left:* The Todd-Bingham Picture Collection, Yale University Library; *bottom right:* Courtesy of The Jones Library, Inc., Amherst, Massachusetts.

p.21 *Top:* Courtesy of The Jones Library, Inc., Amherst, Massachusetts; *bottom:* Photograph by Frank Ward, West Cemetery, Amherst, Massachusetts.

p.22 *Top left:* Courtesy of The Jones Library, Inc., Amherst, Massachusetts; *middle left:* The Dickinson Homestead, Amherst College; photograph by Frank Ward; *bottom left:* Courtesy of Barton St. Armand; photograph by Richard Hurley; *right:* By permission of the Houghton Library, Harvard University.

p.23 The Amherst College Library.

p.24 *Top:* Mead Art Museum, Amherst College, Gift of Arthur D. Norcross; *bottom, both:* By permission of the Houghton Library, Harvard University.

p.25 *Top:* Courtesy of The Jones Library, Inc., Amherst, Massachusetts; *bottom:* By permission of the Houghton Library, Harvard University.

p.26 By permission of the Houghton Library, Harvard University.

p.27 *Top left:* Photograph from *The Life of Emily Dickinson* by Richard Sewall. Copyright © 1974, 1980 by Richard B. Sewall. Reprinted by permission of Farrar, Straus & Giroux, Inc.; *top right:* The Amherst College Library; *bottom left:* Courtesy of Special Collections, The Colorado College Library; *bottom right:* Photograph by Frank Ward, West Cemetery, Amherst.

p.28 *Bottom right:* By permission of the Houghton Library, Harvard University; *all others:* The Todd-Bingham Picture Collection, Yale University Library.

p.29 *Top, both:* The Monson Free Library and Reading Room Association, Monson, Massachusetts; *bottom left:* The Todd-Bingham Picture Collection, Yale University Library; *bottom right:* By permission of the Houghton Library, Harvard University.

p.30 *Both:* Courtesy of The Jones Library, Inc., Amherst, Massachusetts.

p.31 *Top:* The Amherst College Archives; *bottom:* The Amherst College Library.

p.32 *Top:* The Amherst College Library; *bottom:* Courtesy of The Jones Library, Inc., Amherst, Massachusetts.

p.33 Mount Holyoke College Library/Archives.

p.34 Courtesy of The Jones Library, Inc., Amherst, Massachusetts.

p.37 *Both:* Mount Holyoke College Library/Archives.

p.38 *All:* Mount Holyoke College Library/Archives.

p.39 *Top:* The Todd-Bingham Picture Collection, Yale University Library; *middle, bottom:* Mount Holyoke College Library/Archives.

p.40 The Amherst College Library.

p.41 The Monson Free Library and Reading Room Association, Monson, Massachusetts.

p.42 *Top middle:* Photograph from *The Life of Emily Dickinson* by Richard Sewall. Copyright © 1974, 1980 by Richard B. Sewall. Reprinted by permission of Farrar, Straus & Giroux, Inc.; *top left and right:* The Amherst College Archives; *bottom right:* Amherst College Library.

p.43 *Top left:* The Todd-Bingham Picture Collection, Yale University Library; *all others:* By permission of the Houghton Library, Harvard University.

p.44 *Top:* By permission of the Amherst Historical Society, Amherst, Massachusetts; *middle:* Courtesy of The First Church of Christ, Amherst, Massachusetts; *bottom:* By permission of the Houghton Library, Harvard University.

p.45 *Top:* The Todd-Bingham Picture Collection, Yale University Library; *bottom:* By permission of the Houghton Library, Harvard University.

p.46 *Top:* Courtesy of The Jones Library, Inc., Amherst, Massachusetts; *bottom left:* The Forbes Library, Northampton, Massachusetts; *bottom right:* Historic Northampton, Northampton, Massachusetts.

p.47 *Top:* Harvard Law Art collection; *Bottom:* The Todd-Bingham Picture Collection, Yale University Library.

p.48 *Top left and bottom left:* The Amherst College Archives; *top right:* Courtesy of Doheny H. Sessions; *bottom right:* Courtesy of The Franklin Task Library, Andover Newton Theological School.

p.49 *Top left:* Photograph from *The Life of Emily Dickinson* by Richard Sewall. Copyright © 1974, 1980 by Richard B. Sewall. Reprinted by permission of Farrar, Straus & Giroux, Inc.; *top right:* Emily Fowler Ford Papers, Rare Books & Manuscripts Division, The New York Public Library; *bottom left:* By permission of The Amherst Historical Society, Amherst, Massachusetts; *bottom right:* The Amherst College Archives.

p.50 *Top:* Courtesy of Dr. Daniel Bliss; *bottom:* The Amherst College Archives.

p.51 *Top,* and *middle left:* Historic Northampton, Northampton, Massachusetts; *bottom right:* Courtesy of The National Park Service, Springfield Armory National Historic Site.

p.52 *Top left:* Washingtoniana Division, D.C. Public Library; *top right:* The Amherst College Library; *bottom:* The Mount Vernon Ladies Association of the Union.

p.53 *Left:* Courtesy of The Jones Library, Inc., Amherst, Massachusetts; *right:* Photograph from *The Life of Emily Dickinson* by Richard Sewall. Copyright © 1974, 1980 by Richard B. Sewall. Reprinted by permission of Farar, Straus & Giroux, Inc.

p.54 *Top:* Courtesy of The Jones Library, Inc., Amherst, Massachusetts; *bottom:* The Amherst College Library.

p.55 *Top left and right:* Courtesy of The Dickinson Homestead, Amherst College; Photographs by Frank Ward; *bottom:* By permission of the Houghton Library, Harvard University.

p.56 *Top left:* Courtesy of Barton St. Armand; photograph by Richard Hurley; *right:* The Todd-Bingham Picture Collection, Yale University Library; *bottom left:* Courtesy of The Jones Library, Inc., Amherst, Massachusetts.

p.57 *Top:* By permission of the Houghton Library, Harvard University; *bottom:* Courtesy of The Jones Library, Inc., Amherst, Massachusetts.

p.58 *Top:* The Amherst College Library; *bottom:* By permission of the Houghton Library, Harvard University.

p.59 *Top:* By permission of The Amherst Historical Society, Amherst, Massachusetts; *bottom:* By permission of the Houghton Library, Harvard University.

p.60 *Top* and *bottom right:* The Amherst College Archives; *bottom left:* Courtesy of The Pocumtuck Valley Memorial Association, Memorial Hall Museum, Deerfield, Massachusetts.

p.61 *Both:* Courtesy of The Jones Library, Inc., Amherst, Massachusetts.

p.62 Courtesy of The Jones Library, Inc., Amherst, Massachusetts.

p.65 *Both:* The Amherst College Archives.

p.66 Courtesy of The Jones Library, Inc., Amherst, Massachusetts.

p.67 *Both:* Courtesy of The Jones Library, Inc., Amherst, Massachusetts.

p.68 *Top:* Courtesy of Barton St. Armand, photograph by Richard Hurley; *bottom left:* Photograph from *The Life of Emily Dickinson* by Richard Sewall. Copyright © 1974, 1980 by Richard B. Sewall. Reprinted by permission of Farrar, Straus & Giroux, Inc.; *bottom right:* Historic Northampton, Northampton, Massachusetts.

p.69 *All:* By permission of the Houghton Library, Harvard University.

p.70 *Both:* Special Collections, The Colorado College Library.

p.71 *Top left:* Courtesy of Plymouth Church, Milwaukee, Wisconson; *top right:* Courtesy of The Department of History, Presbyterian Church (USA); *bottom:* By permission of the Houghton Library, Harvard University.

p.72 The Amherst College Library.

p.73 *Top:* By permission of the Houghton Library, Harvard; *bottom:* The Amherst College Library.

p.74 *Left:* By permission of the Houghton Library, Harvard University; *Right:* The Amherst College Library.

p.75 *Top:* Courtesy of the Warder Collection; *bottom:* Courtesy of the Trustees of the Boston Public Library.

p.76 *Bottom left:* Courtesy of Amherst College, photograph by Frank Ward; *all others:* The Amherst College Archives.

p.77 *Right:* Courtesy of The Jones Library, Inc., Amherst, Massachusetts; *left:* Courtesy of The American Antiquarian Society.

p.78 *Top:* The Amherst College Archives; *bottom:* Courtesy of the Trustees of the Boston Public Library.

p.79 *Top:* By permission of the Houghton Library, Harvard University; *bottom:* Courtesy of the Boston Athenaeum.

p.80 *Top:* By permission of the Houghton Library, Harvard University; *bottom:* The Dickinson Homestead, Amherst College.

p.81 *All:* By permission of the Houghton Library, Harvard University.

p.82 *Top:* Courtesy of The Jones Library, Inc., Amherst, Massachusetts; *bottom left:* By permission of the Houghton Library, Harvard University; *bottom right:* Courtesy of Barton St. Armand.

p.83 *Top:* By permission of the Houghton Library, Harvard University; *bottom:* The Todd-Bingham Picture Collection, Yale University Library.

p.84 *Top:* Courtesy of Barton St. Armand; *bottom left:* The Dickinson Homestead, Amherst College; *bottom right:* Courtesy of The Jones Library, Inc., Amherst, Massachusetts.

p.85 *Top:* Photograph from *The Life of Emily Dickinson* by Richard Sewall. Copyright © 1974, 1980 by Richard B. Sewall. Reprinted by permission of Farrar, Straus & Giroux, Inc.; *bottom:* The Amherst College Library.

p.86 *Top, and bottom left:* Courtesy of The Jones Library, Inc., Amherst, Massachusetts; *bottom right:* From *Around a Village Green,* by Mary Adele Allen.

p.87 *Both:* Courtesy of The Jones Library, Inc., Amherst, Massachusetts.

p.88 Courtesy of The Jones Library, Inc., Amherst, Massachusetts.

p.91 *Both:* Courtesy of The Jones Library, Inc., Amherst, Massachusetts.

p.92 *Both:* The Amherst College Archives.

p.93 Courtesy of The Jones Library, Inc., Amherst, Massachusetts.

p.94 *Top:* The Amherst College Library; *bottom:* Courtesy of the Trustees of the Boston Public Library.

p.95 By permission of the Houghton Library, Harvard University.

p.96 *Top left:* Courtesy of Barton St. Armand, photograph by Richard Hurley; *top right,* and *bottom:* Courtesy of The Jones Library, Inc., Amherst, Massachusetts.

p.97 *Top:* Courtesy of the National Park Service, Frederick Law Olmsted National Historic Site; *bottom:* Courtesy of The Jones Library, Inc., Amherst, Massachusetts.

p.98 *Left:* By permission of the Houghton Library, Harvard University; *right:* The Todd-Bingham Picture Collection, Yale University Library.

p.99 *Top left:* Special Collections, The Colorado College Library; *top right:* Courtesy of the Folger Shakespeare Library, Washington, D.C.; *bottom:* The Amherst College Library.

p.100 *Top:* Courtesy of The Jones Library, Inc., Amherst, Massachusetts; *bottom:* By permission of the Houghton Library, Harvard University.

p.101 *Top left:* Courtesy of the Dickinson Homestead, Amherst College; *top right:* By permission of the Houghton Library, Harvard University; *bottom left:* Photograph from *The Life of Emily Dickinson* by Richard Sewall. Copyright © 1974, 1980 by Richard B. Sewall. Reprinted by permission of Farrar, Straus & Giroux, Inc.; *bottom right:* The Amherst College Library.

p.102 *Left:* The Todd-Bingham Picture Collection, Yale University Library; *right:* The Amherst College Library.

p.103 *Both:* Courtesy of The Jones Library, Inc., Amherst, Massachusetts.

p.104 *Top:* The Todd-Bingham Picture Collection, Yale University Library; *bottom:* Courtesy of Barton St. Armand.

p.105 Courtesy of The Jones Library, Inc., Amherst, Massachusetts.

p.106 *Both:* The Todd-Bingham Picture Collection, Yale University Library.

p.107 *Top left:* The Todd-Bingham Picture Collection, Yale University Library; *top right:* Courtesy of The Jones Library, Inc., Amherst, Massachusetts; *bottom:* By permission of the Houghton Library, Harvard University.

p.108 *Left:* The Todd-Bingham Picture Collection, Yale University Library; *right:* Mabel Loomis Todd Papers, Manuscripts and Archives, Yale University Library.

p.109 *Top left:* The Todd-Bingham Picture Collection, Yale University Library; By permission of the Houghton Library, Harvard University; *top right:* The Mabel Loomis Todd Papers, Manuscripts and Archives, Yale University Library.

p.110 *Both:* Special Collections, The Colorado College Library.

p.111 *Left:* Photograph from *The Life of Emily Dickinson* by Richard Sewall. Copyright © 1974, 1980 by Richard B. Sewall. Reprinted by permission of Farrar, Straus & Giroux, Inc.; *right:* The Todd-Bingham Picture Collection, Yale University Library.

p.112 *Top left:* Courtesy of The Jones Library, Inc., Amherst, Massachusetts; *top right:* By permission of the Houghton Library, Harvard University; *bottom:* Courtesy of the Douglass Funeral Service, Amherst, Massachusetts.

p.113 *All:* The Amherst College Library.

p.114 Courtesy of The Jones Library, Inc., Amherst, Massachusetts.

p.117 *Both:* The Todd-Bingham Picture Collection, Yale University Library.

p.118 *Both:* The Todd-Bingham Picture Collection, Yale University Library.

p.119 Courtesy of The Jones Library, Inc., Amherst, Massachusetts.

p.120 By permission of the Houghton Library, Harvard University.

p.121 *Left:* Courtesy of Barton St. Armand; *right:* Courtesy of The Jones Library, Inc., Amherst, Massachusetts.

p.122 *Top:* Courtesy of The Jones Library, Inc., Amherst, Massachusetts; *bottom:* The Todd-Bingham Picture Collection, Yale University Library.

p.123 *Top:* Photograph from *The Life of Emily Dickinson* by Richard Sewall. Copyright © 1974, 1980 by Richard B. Sewall. Reprinted by permission of Farrar, Straus & Giroux, Inc.; *bottom:* Photograph by Julie Ainsworth. Courtesy of the Folger Shakespeare Library, Washington, D.C.

p.124 *Top left:* The Amherst College Library; *top,* and *bottom right:* By permission of the Houghton Library, Harvard University; *bottom left:* The Todd-Bingham Picture Collection, Yale University Library.

p.125 *Both:* By permission of the Houghton Library, Harvard University.

p.126 *Top:* Photograph by Frank Ward, Amherst, Massachusetts; *bottom left:* Courtesy of *The Daily Hampshire Gazette,* Northampton, Massachusetts; *bottom right:* Courtesy of Barton St. Armand.

p.127 *Top:* The Todd-Bingham Picture Collection, Yale University Library; *bottom:* By permission of the Houghton Library, Harvard University.
p.128 *Top:* The Dickinson Homestead, Amherst College; *all others:* Courtesy of The Jones Library, Inc., Amherst, Massachusetts.
p.129 *Top:* Photograph from *The Life of Emily Dickinson* by Richard Sewall. Copyright © 1974, 1980 by Richard B. Sewall. Reprinted by permission of Farrar, Straus & Giroux, Inc.; *bottom:* The Amherst College Library.
p.130 *Top:* The Dickinson Homestead, Amherst College, Photograph by Frank Ward; *bottom:* The Dickinson Homestead, Amherst College.
p.131 Photograph by Jerome Liebling.
p.132 Courtesy of the Jones Library, Amherst, Massachusetts.

Index